My Own Worst Enemy

MY OWN WORST ENEMY

BRANDON HEBERT

FIVE STAR
A part of Gale, Cengage Learning

Detroit • New York • San Francisco • New Haven, Conn • Waterville, Maine • London

GALE
CENGAGE Learning™

Copyright © 2009 by Brandon Hebert.
Five Star Publishing, a part of Gale, Cengage Learning.

ALL RIGHTS RESERVED
This novel is a work of fiction. Names, characters, places and incidents are either the product of the author's imagination, or, if real, used fictitiously.

No part of this work covered by the copyright herein may be reproduced, transmitted, stored, or used in any form or by any means graphic, electronic, or mechanical, including but not limited to photocopying, recording, scanning, digitizing, taping, Web distribution, information networks, or information storage and retrieval systems, except as permitted under Section 107 or 108 of the 1976 United States Copyright Act, without the prior written permission of the publisher.

The publisher bears no responsibility for the quality of information provided through author or third-party Web sites and does not have any control over, nor assume any responsibility for, information contained in these sites. Providing these sites should not be construed as an endorsement or approval by the publisher of these organizations or of the positions they may take on various issues.

Set in 11 pt. Plantin.
Printed on permanent paper.

LIBRARY OF CONGRESS CATALOGING-IN-PUBLICATION DATA

Hebert, Brandon.
  My own worst enemy / Brandon Hebert. — 1st ed.
    p. cm.
  ISBN-13: 978-1-59414-827-9 (alk. paper)
  ISBN-10: 1-59414-827-9 (alk. paper)
  1. Street life—Fiction. 2. Miami (Fla.)—Fiction. I. Title.
  PS3608.E284M9 2010
  813'.6—dc22   2009031897

First Edition. First Printing: December 2009.
Published in 2009 in conjunction with Tekno Books and Ed Gorman.

Printed in the United States of America
1 2 3 4 5 6 7 13 12 11 10 09

For Carmen

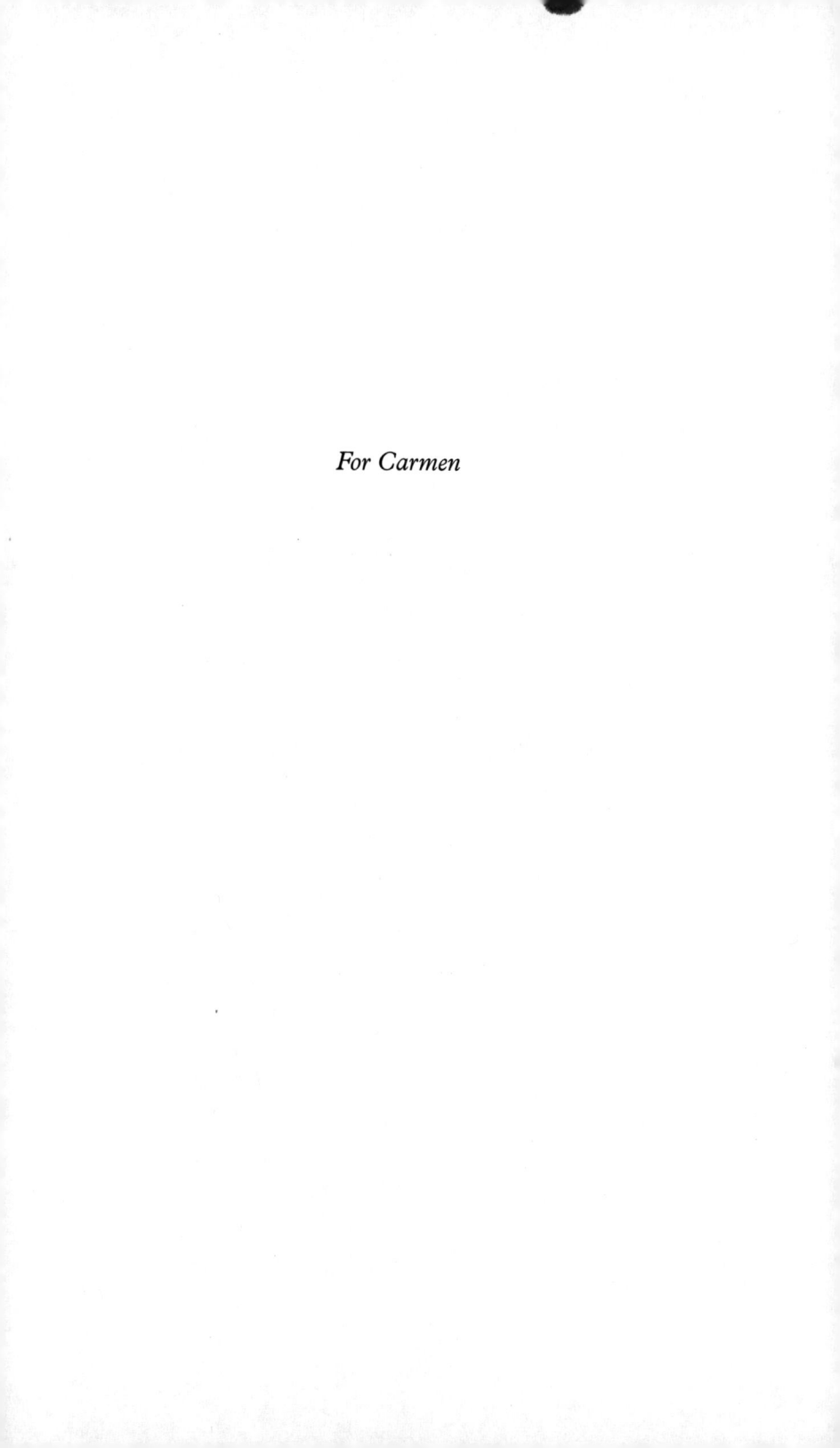

Chapter One

It was funny for Rudy Maxa, watching Jack Murray sitting in the passenger seat, turned partways towards him, rubbing his palms together. He remembered the last time they worked together, watching Jack beat the crap out of Eddie Garza, their third man on that machine shop up in Clewiston. One minute carrying out a roll of copper tubing, man, the next taking a lead pipe to Eddie's shin.

"There it is," Rudy said, going east on El Prado Boulevard.

"That's a big ass house," Murray said, turning his body to see it as the Buick made the round of the cul-de-sac.

Murray was telling himself that he was glad Rudy had this car, an '02 LeSabre, that it was nice enough to fit in, but not nice enough to stand out, thinking that some Gladys Kravitz-type might think it was an out-of-town neighbor or a visitor from some other part of town . . . or the help.

"You sure about this place?"

"Yeah, man," Rudy said, sounding real chummy when he said it, coming close to slapping Murray's leg, "been checking it out for weeks now." He stopped. "Been on top of this one."

Murray felt uneasy, showing it with his jaw clenching, still rubbing the palms.

"Looks like there should be some big time security system," he said.

"There is."

Murray turned around, wanting to put his shoe through Rudy

Maxa's teeth right now but controlling it, saying, "You wait 'til now to tell me this."

Rudy sat there, feeling Murray's stare, the driver's seat starting to swallow him or him shrinking into it, he didn't know or couldn't tell. Just that he was getting fidgety now.

"The old man doesn't know how to work it, though, so it's never on."

Murray seemed unimpressed.

"Look," Rudy shifted in his seat, trying to seem more relaxed, maybe defuse this a little. "Guy's a retired admiral, little old guy, wheeling around his oxygen tank—got a touch of emphysema." He kept at it, saying, "Wife doesn't do much of anything except look after him."

Murray relaxed a little. "You sure he doesn't have anyone come over," he said, the tone lighter, "help him with it?"

Rudy nodded. "I'm sure."

Murray stopped, still not sure about it, extending his arms straight out to touch the dashboard. "How'd you come about this information?"

"I'm tight with their gardener. See, the wife can't do it because the old man's high maintenance, but she's got to keep up with the other yards round here." Rudy looked past Murray to the lawn next door, pointing out the palmettos and sea grape, Murray noticing that some of this yard was a bit overgrown, then hearing Rudy tell him that this gardener friend of his did a couple other properties in this neighborhood.

"I gave him a tip for a Dolphins game one time," Rudy said. "Told him to take the points against New England. Guy thinks I'm Karnack the Great now."

"Yeah, so maybe he's trying for some payback," Murray said. "Maybe grandpa's sitting in there, waiting to bop you over the head with that canister," he kept at it, poking fun, looking for a sore spot. "Get that breathing cord around your neck."

"Look," Rudy said, his voice higher, getting defensive, "no one's home. They went to see Bette Midler at the arena." He calmed down now. "I'm telling you, Jack, it's ready to go."

Murray took a last look around, slash pines blowing in the nighttime breeze, that breeze coming from someplace far away out on the water.

The house was white with the stucco pitched roof, the same stucco on the awnings over the bay windows and the garage. Looking at the house from the driveway, they walked around the left side, in the strip between the side of the house and a privacy fence covered in ivy.

The backyard opened up nicely. The privacy fence continued around the back perimeter of the yard then the rest of the yard, measuring about an acre, maybe a little more, Murray reckoned, keeping it secluded.

Murray inspected the pool for a minute, the water looking soft, bubbles from the jets breaking the plane, distorting the rays of light coming from underneath the surface. The pool was clean, neat, better kept than some of the rest of the ground, Murray thinking they should hire the pool guy to do landscaping from now on.

Murray watched Rudy Maxa move through the patio furniture, following him across the white wicker chairs with tan seat cushions full of pink and purple flowers, to the French doors. At the door, Murray stopped to flip a small backpack from off his shoulder, setting it on the cement.

"What you got?" Rudy said, looking over Murray's shoulder.

Murray didn't say anything, just took out what Rudy could tell through the shadows was a jimmy.

Jack Murray waited. He always hated this part, getting in the door. It was the most nerve-wracking. Even if you were confident about being able to disarm any alarm system, or if it wasn't being used, like Rudy said about the one here, there was still that queasiness about what might happen.

Rudy stood over Murray's shoulder, watching him finesse the jimmy in the doorjam. *Damn. Just do it already*, Rudy forced himself not to say anything out loud.

There it was. The door lock popped. Silence. Just like that. Murray slapped Rudy on the back and stood in the doorway, stopping to get his bearings like he always did when he was somewhere he'd never been before. He followed Rudy through a huge kitchen, then through the adjoining dining room to a hall. The far end was dark, but the end closest to them was lit with a combination of streetlamp and moonlight, the light letting Murray see the bottom of a stairwell.

Rudy Maxa saw Murray start up and followed him. They stopped at the upstairs hall, trying to figure out which room was which.

"Here we go," Murray said, moving right, through the doorframe of what looked to him like the master bedroom.

Murray felt around in his bag for a flashlight, took it out and turned it on. In the dark, he saw the nightstands next to either end of the bed, looking comfy with a big comforter and all those pillows—the pillows probably the wife's idea to dress things up a little. He moved in closer to look at the pictures of the grandkids and . . . felt that maybe he wanted to be somewhere else.

Murray turned when he heard Rudy say he'd found the walk-in closet, the closet that his gardener friend had told him about. Now, how he knew that there was something in there was still fuzzy.

Murray watched Rudy walk in a step, followed him in and felt for a light switch, turning it on to get a look, then turning it off quickly.

They were on their haunches now. All business.

Rudy said, "What's it look like?" trying to sound butch, shifting his weight to see the strong box in the corner, the stainless steel finish reflecting harshly against the flashlight beam.

Murray moved a few pairs of orthopedic shoes and a bedpan aside and felt around the side of the box, getting a hand on either side, then trying half-heartedly to lift. "Bolted," he said, knowing from what he was told that it would be, but wanting to assure himself.

Murray took a few more seconds before saying, "Punch job," half responding to Rudy's question and half just talking out loud, Rudy thinking the tone of voice was distant, like Murray hadn't heard the question and was just saying it for his benefit.

Rudy heard Murray say, "Man," Murray's head turned down, almost at a ninety-degree angle, to get a better vantage point, "this is an old one."

That last part put Rudy at ease, making up for that first part of that statement putting him on alert.

Murray grabbed a ball-peen hammer and punch from his bag. Rudy stopped him, producing his own punch, the metal wrapped in what looked like two coats of rubber, from his pants pocket, saying, "Just did this today," showing off, wanting Murray to think he took his burglarizing seriously.

Murray worked on the keyhole, having to stop to tell Rudy to keep the light where he wanted it, the lock taking two good shots from the chisel before he heard a pop then a metal piece fall, telling him it was loose.

Murray moved the toggle to open the lid, saw the flashlight hit the bound wads of hundred dollar bills—there were three or four of them at first glance—and heard Rudy say "Holy shit" all at what seemed like one moment.

When he finished loading up the backpack with the cash—there were four bound stacks of hundred dollar bills, maybe thirty or forty thousand—Murray looked up and saw the beam of the flashlight bouncing all over the closet. Move up, then stop. Move right. Stop. Move down. Stop.

Murray looked at Rudy Maxa, eyes squinted, letting Rudy see his annoyance. "What're you doing?"

Murray didn't get an answer. Rudy Maxa was too busy getting into the shelf space, too busy pushing aside shoeboxes full of old crap to hear him. He didn't need the answer anyway. You help a guy out, come in on something he's too scared to do by himself, and this is how you're repaid?

The son of a bitch.

This was not how Jack Murray went about his business.

From his crouch, he jerked Rudy's left arm down, the light beam careening all over the walls.

"Knock it off," Murray said, and before Rudy could start, he held an upright index finger to his lips.

"Stick to the job."

Murray didn't feel one way or the other about it; didn't feel guilty about imposing his rule on Rudy Maxa. "Hey, you brought me in on this, remember? You can't do it; you want it done right. Well, don't get greedy. I don't stop you now, where do I stop you? Things like that get out of hand, it's not pretty."

It was on their way down the stairs that Murray saw the flashing lights through the front bay window. He turned to look at Rudy Maxa, Rudy clueless looking at pictures hanging on the stairwell hallway. Murray's first instinct was to get to him. *Put your hands on his shoulders, explain to him what's happening, calm him down before he loses it.* That guy just wasn't built to handle something like this.

Murray turned around and did everything he told himself to do. Hands on the shoulders. Speak slowly. Annunciate.

Didn't help much.

He looked at Rudy, who stood still, with his wide open eyes, upper lip starting to twitch. "Stay here," Murray said, "I'm going to check it out and come back. Okay?"

Rudy nodded his head, Murray nodding his as well.

Murray went down a couple steps, just enough to where he could crouch down to see through a window facing the street.

Shit.

Two of Coral Gables' finest stepped out of a cruiser parked on the curb in front of the yard.

Murray knew they didn't do sweeps until later and that they didn't have call to do them out here anyway.

"We need to go," Murray said, grabbing Rudy's arm and moving back into the master bedroom. He moved to a back window behind the bed that overlooked a small slope of roof then a short fall to the backyard. Murray didn't think twice about it, figuring their only way out was down this way and straight back, over the privacy fence and getting lost in an adjoining neighborhood.

Murray opened the window, removed the screen, and sent Rudy down first, then lowered the backpack and followed. They crouched in the bushes at the side of the house, Murray peeking around the bush, sure that somebody had to come around this way sooner or later.

Rudy took off, Murray trying to get an arm on him, running across the lawn and into some of the brush lining the far corner of the property. He made that run because he had seen shadows move from the front of the house in a direction around the far side, the same way they came in. And he was right.

Murray took off, staying the same course as Rudy Maxa, wondering if the cops around the far side of the house could hear the twigs snapping under his sneakers.

Murray and Rudy Maxa crouched in the bushes lining the yard, their bodies turned to point towards the LeSabre sitting at the curb. The CGPD cruiser was parked at an angle in front of it, but it was nothing to do a quick backup and go around if you did it right. Or, just punch it and try to go around, maybe scrape the bumper.

They didn't talk about what they were going to do. A mistake. Murray went one way, trying to make a run for it over the fence and into the neighbor's yard, thinking if he hit the fence running he could plant his foot halfway up, put his hand on top, and vault over best he could. Rudy went the other way, making his way around the far end of the yard, hidden in the brush, his path to the car clearing when he saw the cops crossing the headlights on their car, running towards Murray.

Rudy was able to back it up and get out quick. Just toss the bag on the passenger seat, turn it on and put it in reverse, quick back in drive and, snap, you're outta there.

Man, that was simple, Rudy told himself. Nothing to it. A lot easier than he thought it would be. He looked in the rearview mirror every couple seconds, smiling to himself at how easy it was to get out of there. Man, always looked so hard in the movies.

Of course, it didn't hurt that both police officers were busy putting Jack Murray on the ground.

Chapter Two

Rudy was always squeamish at the sight of blood. Especially his own when it was going back into the syringe, the time it took for the plunger to extend all the way making him nervous. But, the payoff, wait, one second, two . . . Ah, there it was. *Oh, man, what a feeling.* He slumped back against the wall, shoulders hunching forward. Then, closing his eyes and raising his head. Letting it do its magic.

Rudy felt the needle slide out of his hand, his body too limp to do anything about it. His head moved left, almost an automatic reaction—except that it felt detached from the rest of his body—not really intent on doing anything. He watched Tesha put it in her arm and watched her body react the same way his did. The same lean with the shoulders coming forward then the head cocking back. The eyes rolling to the back of her head. He saw Tesha's legs go straight, shaking a bit, and knew she was way the hell up there. Rudy sat there with his head bobbing, eyes droopy, and thought, *You know, Tesha, you wash your hair and do something with those black circles under your eyes, you might be a good-looking woman.*

"What ya'll doing over there, making goo-goo eyes?" Albert, the guy whose house off Honey Hill Road they were in, said in a kind of drunk or sleepy voice. "Tesha, girl, you best not be kissin' no white boy." Albert tried to get off the floor, break up any lovey-dovey stuff that might've been going on across the room. It wasn't a big room, the living room of Albert's house without furniture but plenty of pillows standing in for chairs, but with his body gooey by now there was no way he was going to make it.

Why was he coming over here anyway? Rudy believed it was because the guy was racist. Rudy was feeling good and loving everybody right now and this guy was trying to ruin his high with that ugliness. Just because he didn't want to see a white and a black getting to know each other under his roof. We're just getting to know each other, that's all. Looking over at Tesha, who was holding her arms across her chest, rubbing them up and down.

Rudy thought that if they weren't so wasted maybe he could tell if Tesha would be better for him than Faye. His old lady. He'd like to know. He only called Faye his old lady because they had been together for so long. Not that they were married or anything. He might like Tesha better, especially if she didn't bitch like Faye did. Bitch and whine. It's what she was best at. It was all that bitching that forced him to start looking around in the first place. It was Faye's fault that he found a new girl. A blonde with an all-over tan and huge tits.

Rudy tried to remember her name.

Jesus Christ, the sound of the knock on the door, somebody banging on it like they were the police, made Rudy jump. Made Albert jump, too. Or at least crawl, trying to reach the .22 tucked under a sofa pillow he was sitting on.

Albert said, "Who that?" bringing the gun up in two shaking hands.

Rudy heard a voice say, "It's Tiras," coming from the other side of the door but sounding like it was far away. Rudy thought about it for a second—as well as he could—but, no, he didn't know anybody named Tiras. Had to be somebody Albert knew, maybe even somebody with reinforcements.

The door opened and *two* guys walked in. Rudy figured Tiras for the taller, leaner of them, the one who started talking to Albert right away. The other one . . . well, "rotund" was the only word that, for some reason, came immediately to Rudy's mind. They seemed to be getting along okay. At least when Rudy opened his eyes they were, the outlines of the two men's frames fuzzy and dark against the faint light of a table lamp on the floor next to Albert.

Rudy couldn't hear what they were saying but, look at them, talking like old friends. Fucking Albert. Ashamed to introduce a white guy to your old friends. He started to drift in and out, losing consciousness every so often, hoping this Tiras would hurry up and break out the stuff he had for his old buddy Albert. Now, Rudy couldn't be totally sure of this last part because it happened right as he blacked out for a minute. But, he could have sworn he saw Albert's old friend Tiras take out a gun and shoot Albert in the head.

"Tesha, girl, you don't look so good," the one named Tiras said.

Tesha looked bug-eyed at Albert laying on the floor across from her. Her body tightened, fists coming over her head as she said, "What you want?" before curling into a fetal position.

She said it again, this time the voice coming from some nether region, and Tiras said, "You know what I'm here for."

Tesha unraveled her body, straightened out and started to undo her shirt, hands shaking at each button.

"Girl, puhleeze." Tiras made a disgusted face. "You think I ain't got nothing better to do than bang a skank like you?" He shook his head as he watched Tesha pull her shirt closed, holding it to her body.

Tiras said, "I'm going to count to three," and raised a .45 to her head.

Tesha's head moved side to side, doing anything to avoid looking at the gun pointed at her. Tiras had reached two and was about to open his mouth again when she said, "I think he keeps some in the freezer."

"The freezer, huh?" Tiras brought the .45 down and turned to the other man and said, "Go on and check."

Rudy saw a light from the kitchen come on behind Tiras. Then, he saw Tiras look right at him. He thought Tiras might shoot *him*. But, he just stared. Feeling Tiras's look until they heard footsteps, Tiras's sidekick moving dining table chairs out of the way coming back from the kitchen.

The other man, the rotund one, handed Tiras a brick of cash in freezer wrap and said, "I bet there's fifteen thousand in there." Tiras held it up, turning it around to look at it from different angles. The other man said, "You can see there's lots of hundreds and fifties in there."

Tiras said, "That's pretty good," still looking at it. He raised the .45 and pulled the trigger. Without looking, no big deal. Tesha's body smacked against the wall and held there.

Rudy watched Tesha's head slump forward, chin hitting her chest. Then, her upper body tilt towards him. "How you like that?" Tiras said when Tesha's head landed in Rudy's lap. "She ain't dead, you might get a blowjob."

Tiras and the other one laughed at his joke, and Tiras got on his haunches, saying, "What's your name, man?"

"Rudy." Sounding alert and awake when he said it.

Tiras nodded, looking like he was taking a minute to figure out what to do with this Rudy character. He said, "What you doing here?"

Rudy shrugged, nodding like he was caught doing something and was upset with himself.

"You prob'ly think that's a stupid question, huh," Tiras said. "I mean, it's obvious what you doing here."

Rudy didn't say anything, sure that it was a one-sided conversation. He brought his legs up close to his body and started shaking.

"Don't worry," Tiras said, standing up and backing away. "You ain't gonna feel a thing."

It probably happened fast, but there was enough time for Rudy to think. Time enough to think about a way out of this mess. Fucking Albert, always something with him. If it wasn't his racist ways, then it was some fucking drug dealer he pissed off coming in and killing everybody for his revenge.

It surprised Rudy, his mind being clear enough to process thoughts. That had never happened to him before when he was high. Funny things happen when you have a gun in your face.

"I can give you something," Rudy said.

"What, if I let you live?"

Rudy let it hang, not wanting to let the man know that, *Yeah, to let me live*, was what he was thinking.

Tiras shrugged and nodded at the same time. Waiting. "Well?"

"Seventy thousand dollars."

See if that does it.

Tiras nodded. "Where this seventy thousand at?"

"Not here."

Tiras smiled and brought the .45 down to his side. He said, "No, I guess it's not."

"It's at my girlfriend's house."

Tiras slapped the other man in the belly with the back of his hand and said, "Big man here's got seventy thousand at his girlfriend's house," still looking at Rudy. He looked around the room before saying, "You such a big man, what you doing in a shithole like this?"

Rudy didn't have an answer for that.

Tiras didn't seem to mind, or notice, because he said, "Where you get that kind of money anyhow, big shot?" right away. Like it was something he forgot to ask before.

Rudy said, "It's the take off some old jobs." Getting brave

now. Tiras called him a player, and Rudy took it to mean they were getting to be old friends now.

Just like with Albert.

Rudy started talking. Talking too much—about the job with Jack Murray, about some other jobs, about his old partner that lived in Atlanta now that he was hooking up with on a major score. He stopped to emphasize the word *major*.

Tiras asked him what kind of score—okay, if this white bread wanted to use that word—and Rudy said, "We're going to use that money to buy some guns and turn them around to some buyers he has lined up. Some Venezuelans. Make some big money."

"You mean my seventy thousand dollars?" Tiras looked into the white bread's eyes and saw that there was some recognition of what was happening.

Sure of it when he saw the white bread's shoulders slump and eyes look toward the floor.

"Don't look so sad, Rudy." Tiras took a second, almost forgetting the name. "You spend all that money, that's a lot of guns. You would've needed help anyway."

The day he got out of Okeechobee Correctional Institution, Jack Murray remembered when his Uncle Merrill sat him down and said, "Son, the minute you get emotional about those you're stealing from, you're done." Then, he watched his uncle tilt back in his easy chair, pushing his cowboy hat back to the crown of his head and heard him say, "True, your uncle's maybe had some misgivings," Murray had been doing it long enough, even at seventeen by that time, to know it was more than a few, "about some good folk he might've done wrong." Then, Merrill shot straight up in his chair. "But, they could handle it. All of them. Don't ever take more than you know they can stand to lose." He paused, mostly for effect. "You wanna stay in the game, you remember that."

He'd forgotten until recently. It was a real wake up in court. The circuit court judge, criminal division, for Dade County really raked him over the coals for this one. A lady. Whew. By the time she got done, all Murray could think of was that one Flintstones cartoon where Mister Slate was yelling at Fred, and Fred just got smaller and smaller and smaller. When it was over, Fred was about a half-inch from the floor. Man, what really hurt him is that the guy before him was up there for killing seven puppies. He got it worse but following that was not easy.

Murray heard the audience lose it when she said out loud that the victim was ninety-one-years-old. And on oxygen supply, although Murray knew that part. Hell, he had a gap-toothed, greasy-faced woman whose husband had just been arraigned for kicking an eight-year-old in the head getting after him. Damn.

The judge had to bang the gavel to get order back after she said that the twenty-three thousand five hundred sixty-eight dollars in question was for medical expenses. All they had left.

Murray's only saving grace was that he wasn't inside the house when he was arrested. Plus, the public defender watered down the prosecution's argument, saying that his client had no tools obvious for burglarizing on him and none of the money in question. Still, he wasn't going to cooperate about naming a co-conspirator (their word)—another rule of his—so they'd split it down the middle. Bottom line was he'd do not less than one year and one day instead of four years.

Another thing he'd never really given much thought to until today, mostly a conscious decision of his but it was starting to nag at him was . . .

Whatever happened to Rudy Maxa and all that money?

Tommy Smalls said to Jack Murray, "Good to be out, huh?"

Murray didn't say anything, Tommy's voice barely registering. He didn't say anything since they left Okeechobee and got onto 441, then onto 710 and now on 95, going south, passing Deerfield Beach. Just sat there, sometimes bored, sometimes replaying in his head what got him to this point, staring out at the highway, the high rise apartment buildings, watching how flat some of the undeveloped parts were. His eyes moved away from the window, by habit checking the speedometer, Tommy Smalls holding it between fifty-five and sixty, hoping for a smooth ride back. Sometimes, a guy gets out, his ride home is a madman on the road, man, look out. If you're the ride home, you mind your p's and q's on the road. Make it uneventful.

Tommy said, "So what you want to do first?" He felt Murray staring at him, though when he looked over at him, Murray looked away and was stretching his legs out, the soles of his shoes pressing hard against the floorboard.

"What're you talking about?"

Tommy could feel Murray staring at him again. He lit a cigarette, a single he had in his shirt pocket. "I dunno," he said, playing it off.

He took a long drag and let it rip. "Some guys get out, they got to get back to their specialty right away," flicking his ash out of the window, "thinking they're out of practice. I read in the paper about this one guy, guy was robbing banks out in Ohio, did a job like," he had to remember it, "two hours after he got out." Tommy slammed the steering wheel before he said, "Bam!" Then, "Gets sent back same day."

Murray shook his head, making a face. "So, you think I want to go break into somebody's house?" He turned to Tommy. "Right now?"

Tommy waved his hand, trying to dismiss it, trying not to annoy further. "Was just a thought."

Murray, wondering about this guy, said, "Tommy, don't think, okay."

Murray let it drop, let it stay quiet, take advantage of the quiet to gather his thoughts. "I'm through with that anyway."

"With what?"

"Everything."

"The life?"

Murray nodded his head, laughing a little at that one, Tommy watching *Goodfellas* one too many times.

"Yeah," he said, looking down, still grinning, "the life."

Tommy shook his head, a pained expression coming over his face, whistling through his teeth. "How come?"

Murray sat up, hoping that it might help Tommy to comprehend.

"Tommy, I just spent a year-and-a-day in jail," he searched for the words to finish, "when I shouldn't have been there in the first place." His body fell, the energy gone from explaining himself. "I'm tired."

"You know," Tommy said, "I saw where they did a survey once, fifty percent of the guys that commit crimes are out of it by the time they're forty. You're what thirty-five, thirty-six. So, there's a fifty percent chance you only got four or five years left."

"What happened to the other half?" Murray said, not looking at Tommy, slumping in his seat, closing his eyes.

Tommy shrugged. "I'm not sure. Don't believe they said." Tommy was nervous now, knowing that he was screwing up, not with his driving like he told himself not to, but in other ways, asking too many questions. "All's I'm saying, you got a little time left, then you're practically retired. Don't fuck it up, piss the wrong people off. Okay?"

Tommy heard Jack Murray grunt and say something to himself that he couldn't make out.

Tommy said, "Well, if you're tired, you can rest up at my place."

Murray didn't want to get into it too much more, knowing Tommy meant well. He could empathize. Tommy was probably on the road by seven in the morning, probably taking an hour and change to get up to Okeechobee. Then, another hour while Murray was processed, fucking c.o.s dragging their feet with his gate money. Then, traffic picking up on the way back, getting thicker the further south they got. Nearing noon now.

He didn't want to get into it because sooner or later he was going to explode, and he didn't want to do that. It was his first day out. There'd be plenty of time for that. Murray sat up in his seat again, steeling himself for five more minutes of conversation, really bring it home for Tommy.

"I don't think you get it," he said. "I'm tired of breaking into people's houses, tired of stealing cars, tired of worrying about the police all the time. And, I sure as hell don't want to go back there." Saying it, Murray hoped Tommy knew he meant Okeechobee, or any facility for that matter.

Murray was sure that Tommy got it, or as much as he could right now. Drained from the questions, he wondered if jail really wasn't better than this car ride until Tommy said, "How can you say that? Caesar's always taken good care of you." Tommy stopped for almost a minute, taking time to pick a piece of tobacco off his tongue, using the time to gather his thoughts. "You're not all the way Italian, jeez, neither am I, but he still treats us like family."

Murray relaxed back in his seat, not bothering to look at Tommy when he spoke, relieved that they were coming on the Fort Lauderdale exits. "And, I'll be sure to thank him for it." Then, in a tone not sounding like the hard ass ex-con. "But, this isn't about Caesar."

It was quiet while Tommy concentrated on not passing up his

exit, his eyes straight ahead, both hands on the wheel, turning it hand over hand through the curved off ramp until they were heading east on West Broward.

"Maybe he'll have something light for you, huh?"

Murray didn't say anything.

But, Tommy said, "Maybe at the track, watch the races, collect, maybe look after one of his fighters, something like that."

Murray made a noise, Tommy not sure what it meant but probably that Murray didn't believe him.

"Well," Tommy said, "he wants to see you anyway."

Their boss, if Murray could call him that because he let Murray do his own thing most of the time, Caesar Pelli, had a beautiful sixty-footer at American Marina, Bahia Mar. Called it "Wild Thing." Seventy-years-old and he calls his boat something like that. Huh. Guy just never grew up.

Murray had been on the boat a few times, mostly for parties. They'd cruise down the coast and park off South Beach, let the sun go down and watch the lights on all the hotels, letting that go on in the background while they had their fun. Always some blondes onboard, Murray figuring some of them were the goumadas, if they still used that word. Some there to hang on the men, the capos, and live the lifestyle, laughing at all the bad jokes or all the punch lines on stories they didn't know anything about. Guess with friends like that you don't have to grow up.

They were here now. Through the open sliding doors leading into the lounge, Murray saw two bikini blondes giving Caesar a rubdown. Seeing Caesar relaxed like this, telling one of his beauties where to rub, gave Murray pause. He'd rehearsed it in his head but seeing the man, here in the flesh after such a long time, made it difficult.

When Caesar inherited the operation from some of the old world bosses, Murray was just a kid, still in short pants. It was his old man, Jim, who came up through the ranks; keeping his books, collecting on debts, running his sheets out of Gulfstream. Eventually, his dad put in enough time to where he just made sure guys were where they were supposed to be, coordinating. You're supposed to be picking up boxes of stereos fell off a truck in Homestead, well, you damn well better be there. Your girlfriend's sick, and you have to take her to the doctor? What, in the middle of the night? Fuck you, be there.

So, when they came out of Wolfie's one night, and his old man bought it jumping in front of a bullet meant for Caesar, Murray was offered his spot. Murray had been on his own for a while, without much success. So, go from getting lollipops as a kid to a hundred grand in seed money and the option to keep freelancing a little. Hard to turn away.

Tommy Smalls said, "Here he is, boss," trying to act like a big brother, like it was a homecoming.

Caesar threw his hands up, saying "Jackie."

Still calling him that. Like he was nine.

Murray held his arms out, hugging the old man, and said, "How are you, Caesar?"

Caesar Pelli shook his head, threw his arms up, frowned, all in that animated way he had about him. Without really answering the question. Finally, "I'm fine, Jackie." He stopped, a quizzical look coming over his face. "The real question is, how are you?" Slapping Murray's arm, he said, "Didn't turn sissy on us, did you?"

Murray shook his head, trying to laugh, remembering the fat Aryan motherfucker that came at him in the shower his first week. A swift kick to the nuts followed by a jab to the breastbone and a crew of Murray's boys in there already solved that.

Caesar stood there, broad smile, in a hunched pose, head down, shoulders up, like he was still waiting for that answer. When Murray didn't say anything, maybe just mouthed a no and shook his head again, the old man jumped up and hugged him again, glad to see him.

He pinched Murray's cheek, bringing their faces close together. "You're a good boy, Jack. You don't roll over on anything they could've asked you about." Caesar getting serious now, putting his hand on Murray's shoulder, saying, "Took your time like a man," that serious look on his face, too.

"It was totally unrelated to anything we're doing," Murray said.

"I know," pause, "I know," Caesar said, still worried, though. "But it's always good to see one of my boys keep his mouth shut when he's in a pinch. It's good business, Jackie. Speaks highly of you."

Chrissakes, the mood getting real serious, almost sappy now.

Murray wanted to lighten it up a bit, set the old man up for his fastball right down the middle.

Murray thought about it, relying on an old standby, "So you can brag about me, huh?"

That brought it out in Caesar, the little shrinking, almost-hunchback old man body rocking back and forth now, laughing.

"Hey," he said, "don't make fun. Other day, we were playing cards out at Doral, some jackass real estate guy says, 'My kid just got into Harvard.' 'Hey,' I turn around and say, 'Yeah, my boy's getting out of the shitcan.' "

Murray didn't want to drag it out, thinking the old man was softened up. "Look, Caesar . . ." he said, the tone giving away that something was coming, "I wanted to come by, tell you that I appreciate everything you've done for me but . . ."

"Wait a minute," Caesar said, hand on his head like he was trying to understand. "Wait a goddamn minute. What's this 'but' crap? But what?"

"Well, I've had a lot of time to think things over," he searched for a something to sum it up, sound good, "to re-evaluate," good one, "and I just don't know if I can do it anymore."

Caesar paced, trying to figure out how to take the news. Best he could come up with was to go over to Tommy Smalls, who had been sitting on a deck chair eyeing one of the girls, trying to get her number, and give him an open palm upside the head. "You?" Caesar said, the hand still up. "You been talking to him, talking this shit?"

Tommy just sat there, mouth open, dumb look on his face. "What?" he said, rubbing his head. "I didn't have nothing to do with it," Caesar started to walk away, leaving Tommy talking to the back of the old man's head now. "I picked him up like you told me. He starts talking this way."

Caesar calmed down a bit, walking up to Murray, putting his squinting gaze into Murray's face. "So, what exactly are you talking about, Jackie?"

"I want to try and stay clean," Murray said, wondering how pathetic it sounded.

"Jackie," Caesar turning chummy again, "you been working for me since you were a pup, a little guy." He put a straight hand out, pressing it against himself at mid-thigh, trying to tell him how tall Murray was when they met.

"You're making this real hard, Caesar."

Caesar brought Murray over to a leather deck sofa, sitting him down and ordering up two brandys from one girl he called Mandy.

"This should be hard, Jack," Caesar playing father figure now, putting his hand on Murray's knee. "This is a major life decision you're making."

Caesar sat back, Mandy serving up their drinks. "Look, Jack," always Jack now, "I understand. One time, I remember, I went in," he leaned into Murray, telling him as an aside that he spent time at Glades in seventy-three, "I came out in a funk. I didn't want to talk to anybody, didn't want to see anybody, didn't want anything to do with any of them. I was spooked." Caesar concentrated on his snifter. "It's just a phase."

"Look, Caesar . . ." Murray said, not really knowing where he was going with it. He didn't have a plan, which was part of the trouble. You go to the boss, tell him you want out, then what, tell him you'll flip burgers at McDonald's until something comes along?

"Jack," Caesar said, "you say you want to go clean, get respectable, then clean it is. I can respect that."

Murray jumped back, surprised.

Caesar put his hand on Murray's shoulder again. "Hey, don't let this get around, okay?"

Murray nodded, appreciating.

"You're a special case to me, Jackie," he said, the eyes wandering off, starting to get lost in some different time, long ago, then regrouping. "Look, I got this club on Collins. I'm looking for a manager. You go by there tomorrow night 'cause you're it." Then, "Get some managerial work under your belt. Put it on your resume."

Murray wasn't sure if he liked the feel of it, this discussion not going as smooth as he'd hoped. He held up a hand, making one of those earnest frowns like he was really contemplating, wanting to say thanks but no thanks.

"Jack," Caesar said, "it's all I can offer right now. It won't satisfy your p.o., but we'll get around that, don't you worry." He held up one of his big knobby fingers. "And, it's legit in there, I guarantee you. I don't allow no funny business in there. You got a club, you're already under a microscope, so anything happens in there," Caesar heard the slip, "It's controlled. I don't let it happen 'cause you'll lose your liquor license quicker than shit. You know how much cash liquor brings in, a joint like that? You think I'm gonna risk that?"

Caesar could see Murray waffling on it, rocking his head

back and forth like it was a pro or con each time his head went a different way.

"It'll tide you over until you make a definite decision, get yourself up and running."

Murray nodded, Caesar happy.

"Good," the old man said, putting his hand around Murray's collar. "Tommy'll take you over," he turned to Tommy, "tomorrow night, okay?" Then, back to Murray. "You go get cleaned up, Jack. Wash the jail off you. It'll do you some good."

Caesar Pelli watched Jack Murray and Tommy Smalls walk off the deck, down the pier and back towards the marina office, losing sight of them as they got to the parking lot when Mandy called him back into the lounge, on the staircase going below decks.

Ten in the morning. Light coming through the window woke Murray up. He took a minute to rub his eyes, taking a long look at the lime green wall paint and arching his back because his sleep wasn't too comfortable in the tiny bed with the scratchy comforter and too firm pillow.

He'd gotten a one-bedroom apartment at the Casita Guest House for five hundred bucks a month through the low season, a favor called in by Caesar while he shopped for his own place. Murray got out of bed, the tile floor cool against his bare skin. He moved the shade a bit, looking out in an alley that came off Collins. His room was at the end of the alley, away from the noise, mostly because the manager wanted to keep rooms near the street for the tourists. But, he thought he was lucky, being back here seemed like it would be almost quiet most nights. Hey, walking distance to his new job and a block from Ocean Drive and the beach and better furnished than his last place, what with the cinder block entertainment center and all. For five hundred bucks a month? Not too bad.

For the first time he could remember, Murray wanted to meet his neighbors. There were a few regulars at the Casita, and he could see them, already outside, a group of bluehairs gathering on the rattan benches with the floral print pillows. He thought about going down there, introducing himself, playing the politico, glad-handing, kissing the old ladies on the cheek. No, make a big splash. He wanted to make them some lunch. He felt like an omelet himself, but it would be noon at the earliest before he even got back from the Publix on Alton.

What he decided to do was clean up, introduce himself to the group, and fix them supper. He got some sideways glances at first, the old gents wondering if he was trying to put the make on their late-in-life girlfriends, and the old gals wondering if he was trying to lift their handbags then run down the street, like Seinfeld stealing that old lady's marble rye.

They were where they said they would be come four o'clock, wanting to eat and be back in time for *Wheel of Fortune* or *Jeopardy!*, when Murray brought down a tray of Havana omelets in one hand and some TV trays under his other arm.

It put Jack Murray in a different place, listening to Earl the butcher talk about what Miami Beach used to be. How Arthur Godfrey and Jackie Gleason would personally—and he stressed that part—come in for his pork tenderloin cut; listening to Marjorie talk about working on a B-52 assembly line in 1942. Agnes, the other, didn't say much unless they started talking about what time they took their pills.

Murray watched the ladies take small bites, waiting for one of them to look up and give him a sign that it was good. They ate like birds. Agnes, between bites and her opinion on the state of Medicare, turned to him, saying, "This is delicious."

Murray nodded, happy to hear his cooking passed muster. He moved his eyes over to Earl, his head buried in the plate, Murray wondering when he was going to come up for air.

Earl was talking now, making the ladies laugh with some line about the tourists passing on Collins. The guy talking it up, putting his charm out there, protecting his turf in case Murray, the young whippersnapper, had designs on his women. "So, Jack," he said between bites, then finishing up before he started again, "what do you do for a living?"

There it was. He looked at them. Earl, Marjorie, and Agnes, giving their interested stares, ready to judge if they didn't like his line of work.

"Insurance." Murray blurted it out. It was the first thing that came across his mind, remembering *Double Indemnity* on the tube last night. He hoped they didn't see it and think he was the Fred MacMurray-type insurance man. Scheming. Still, tell them you're fresh out of jail, they think they're living next to a gangster wondering if you're hanging out with other gangsters doing a lot of gangster shit.

Murray hoped they wouldn't press. If they asked what kind, he'd have to fumble for it. How many different insurances were there? They didn't, though. The ladies took back to their bird bites. Earl back to talking about how many celebs he hobnobbed with in the old days.

"You know," Murray said, "if you want, I bet you could catch Paris Hilton around here somewhere." He took a chance with it, wondering if they thought he was being a smart ass, some punk trying to have a laugh at their expense.

Earl laughed it off, then turned serious, saying, "Yeah," pulling at his belt loop, "if I was eight hundred years younger." Meaning it, too.

Murray turned, enjoying himself, watching the sun through a strip of buildings go lower over the Atlantic when Tommy Smalls's silhouette showed up against the glare, coming down the alley off Collins. Oh, man, this was embarrassing. All the goodwill . . . gone. Murray trying to build a rapport here, trying to make new friends—even if they would have been his mom or dad's age—wiped away by Tommy's oily hair, slicked back, long over the ears and in back. All Murray could remember was the story his old man would tell him about his grandpa shitting a brick when The Beatles showed up on Ed Sullivan. Or, the day-old growth, Tommy obviously not shaving today. He just didn't look like the kind of guy a respectable insurance man should be hanging around with.

"Jack," Tommy said, the cigarette hanging from his right hand, a grin coming over his face.

Murray was turning pink going through the introductions, trying to hurry it up so he could get Tommy upstairs, out of sight. He was getting up to collect the TV trays when he heard Tommy say . . .

"Jack, shouldn't you be getting dressed for work?"

Chapter Three

Funny how the guys in the club always thought the girls gave a damn about them. They were just money. Murray knew this. He couldn't understand how so many others didn't realize this as well. Always breaking out twenties, thinking that they were buying love. Some did indeed know the score, but the majority were clueless as hell.

This wasn't a bad gig as gigs go for Jack Murray. Two-time losers normally do much worse than this. Thank God he had family. Rewards for stir were inconsistent. All depended on your disposition. Jack, when was the last time you used a word that big? Was that the right one? Better look it up later—before using it in conversation.

If you were naughty, which meant you either turned sissy or you talked, well, you'd get yours. If you were nice, you might get taken care of. Might. Might mostly meant busting your ass at some bullshit job to keep the parole officer happy. Murray was nice. He didn't figure he was this nice. Manager of a strip club. Jeez, you got to be high up to get this. He was told to check it out, see if he liked it. This was not an audition, though. They knew he would like it. He wasn't full-blood family, but Caesar had always kept an eye on him. Murray felt embarrassed sometimes, still living off his old man's honor. Caesar didn't think twice, though. Good fella, that Caesar.

The gin and tonic that Tommy had ordered for him arrived. Tommy was already nursing some red, fruity drink. Thankfully there wasn't some gay umbrella fondling the rim of the glass.

An hour in, Murray felt himself falling back into place, getting jazzed about this. He liked the location, at 20th and Collins—the old Showgirls. There was a video store next door. Buy that, gut it, show some nudie pictures, maybe a peep show for a change of pace.

"See her?" Tommy said, pointing to the stage with his glass in hand, index finger extended.

Murray nodded. He watched the brunette slide up then down on the stage pole, wrap one leg around and pull some backwards bend so the john could tuck a five-spot in her cleavage. They went nuts. The rest of the jackals weren't far behind, dropping fives, tens, twenties, ones, whatever. Jack envisioned her eyes like in the old cartoons, dollar signs where the pupils are supposed to be.

"That's Cindy," Tommy, shaking his head, said. "She's a mother of two. Cutest little guys."

Murray's brow rose. Impressive. She didn't look like any mother of two that he had ever seen. Cindy was up there, smiling a lot, looking like she was having a good time, really enjoying it. Murray wondered about her kids, if they knew where their mommy was right now. Or the husband if there was one.

"And her." Tommy pointed to the stage beyond Cindy. It was a pretty blonde, well built. She was almost built enough to be on some circuit. Some guys were into that. Murray decided long ago that he didn't care for it. "That's Sidney. Or Sid. Anyway, she's my hairdresser."

Murray glanced at Tommy's head. Could've used an appointment about three hours ago. It was coifed in some places, but damn, he didn't keep it well enough to need a "hairdresser."

Tommy gave Murray a look that said, *What the hell?* He patted his head, self-conscious now.

A redhead had taken Cindy's place by now. She was strutting

hard in a red, white and blue bikini. He liked her timing, throwing the curtain open to the throaty warble at the top of "Hit and Run Holiday." As soon as she ripped her top off, the place exploded. Murray loved patriotism.

"That," Tommy pointed at Miss Fourth of July, "is Simone. Twenty. Sophomore at Dade County. She's using this to pay off her convertible VW."

"I like a good work ethic."

Murray sat there on his stool, concentrating, liking the girls that he was watching right now, but some of them, uh, left something to be desired. Cotton panties and pasties covering the parts they didn't want under too much scrutiny. Some tired looking broads trying to make that buck that came so easy to girls like Cindy and Simone. That would be another thing to look in to. Girls. Some had to be downsized. Especially if he was going to make a name here. Really shake it up. Girls that weren't bothering the customers for a dollar every time they walked by. That brought the novelty factor way down. And, funny that the worst offenders were the ones who didn't get it working the stage. Getting close enough to stick your sagging tits in some guy's face wasn't going to improve your odds any. Get some girls with hard asses and no cottage cheese.

Murray turned to nurse his drink, elbows on the bar, the stage reflecting in the mirrored bar wall. The emcee was onstage. He was never on for long, just enough to buy time before the next round of ladies, but the johns weren't ready for his crap. He was getting booed off, and loud.

"I'm going take a look around," Murray said turning to Tommy.

"Yep." Tommy's stare didn't break from the stage.

Backstage was very busy. Murray made his way through the crowd, nodding to the crew. They returned the nods, not really knowing who the hell he was. He wasn't even sure where he was going.

There was a door. He knocked.

"Who is it?" The voice was sexy.

Murray was demure, poking his head through the door. If he got caught copping a look at least he didn't want to make it look obvious. The Voice was alone. Staring at him in the reflection of the makeup mirror.

"Sorry. Just wanted to check and see if you needed help getting ready." It was lame. He knew it.

"And you are?" She was a little pissed off, giving Murray the valley girl lip snarl.

His steps through the door were delicate. He was already close to being laughed out of the room. "Jack Murray. I'm going to be the new manager here."

"Really?" She turned, showing off the short blonde bob, bronze skin, perfectly white teeth. The Figure matched The Voice.

"Yeah." Murray plunged in. "What's your name?" He nodded his head when he said it, like it was old hat, trying to look cool.

"Shelly."

"Shelly what?"

"Shelly Suxxx."

Murray's head jerked back.

"Actually, it's only my stage name." She flashed The Teeth.

"Well, what's your real name?" Maintain the cool.

"Miranda."

Murray tilted his head forward, expecting more.

"Miranda Mendoza."

Murray mouthed 'Miranda' to himself. The cool was starting to slip. "That's a beautiful name." Good recovery.

"Well, Jack, it's very nice to meet you."

Murray nodded.

"What exactly did you say you were going to be doing here?" Miranda said.

"I'm going be the new manager."

"Really?"

Again, Murray nodded. Big man. He felt himself getting comfortable with her, deciding to take the conversation further. "So, what do you do outside of this?" He thought it was a good entry, seeing as how, according to Tommy's description, this was part-time for almost all the girls here, working towards something else.

"College. Florida Atlantic."

Murray nodded, looking interested.

"Psych major."

Oh, dear. Murray's look changed, becoming visible that he was waiting for Psych 101 to rear its ugly head, waiting for her to turn this into some encounter group.

"Don't worry," she said, "I'm third year."

So, she did read his mind.

"Plus, I'm twenty-six. So, I'm a little beyond trying to dissect everyone I come into contact with."

He wondered if she could tell what he was thinking right now.

Murray glanced at his watch, still wanting to get it over before she tried to delve too deep. "What time do you go on?"

"Actually, I'm done." Miranda motioned to her stage clothes hanging on the rolling rack. "I was just getting ready to meet some girlfriends." She batted her eyes. "I hope you don't mind. I mean, me getting ready here and all."

"Not at all."

"Thank you."

"Well," Murray thumbed toward the door, "I need to get going. It was good meeting you, though."

"You, too." Miranda turned back to apply her blush, staring at Murray's reflection in the mirror.

Back in the main parlor, Murray's sixth sense kicked in, looking beyond a table of conventioneers having a good time, past the male tourists running around on their wives or girlfriends, hoping their buddies would keep quiet when they got back to Wisconsin.

Murray tapped Ed, otherwise known as Big Black Bouncer, on the shoulder. Not too hard. You didn't want Ed thinking you were some wiseass starting trouble and take your head off with arms roughly the size of tree trunks.

Ed turned. "Wassup, boss?"

"See that white guy over there?" Murray pointed to a table away from the stage on the second tier. "With those two black guys?"

"Yeah. What about them?"

"What do you know about the black fellas?"

"Those two? Fuckin' whack jobs, boss. That one . . ." Ed pointed to the tall, thin one, ". . . name's Tiras Williams. He suppose to be some kinda badass. Into guns . . . drugs . . . white women. Whatever."

"What about the fat one?"

"That fatass? Goes by Lil' Man, only I dunno why they call him that. Fatter than hell. Anyway, his sole purpose on earth is to watch the other one's back."

Murray pursed his lips in surprise.

"Dunno jack," Ed excused himself of the pun, "about white bread that's with them, though."

"That's okay. I do."

"Yeah? What's his deal?"

"He's the reason I just spent three hundred sixty-six days in jail."

Murray didn't think they were Rudy's crowd.

"Rudy?"

The white bread's head whipped. "I thought you were busted, man."

Murray took a minute to look Rudy Maxa over, running his hand down the lapel of Rudy's suit jacket. He was too skinny for it. Still, Murray decided to play it up. "Looks like you're doing real good for yourself." He stooped to look Rudy in the eye. "What's wrong? Not happy to see me?"

"There a problem?" It came from behind Murray's left ear.

Murray turned, getting an up close look at Tiras Williams: Tall, shiny bald head, real put together in a six-foot frame, eyes bright in the neon. "No problem." Murray straightened Rudy's collar point. "I was just talking to Rudy."

"Well, Rudy belong to me. So, anybody talking to Rudy," Tiras double-tapped his chest, "talking to me."

"So, he didn't tell you?"

They were back in the yard, sizing each other up. Nobody backing down. Didn't want to back down, or you'd be face down. Bad impression meant you could wake up dead. Didn't feel much different on the outside, at least not in this line of work.

Tiras gave Rudy a slow burn. "Tell me what?"

"Uh," Rudy stepped in, giving his two cents, "Ty, this is Jack Murray." Rudy waved his arm back and forth between Murray and Tiras, like he was expecting them to shake and make nice.

Murray waited for Rudy to say something. He didn't. Hell with it. "We used to work together," he said, knowing it would aggravate the situation.

Rudy nodded. Looked like a five-year-old, hanging his head,

getting reamed for having his hand in the cookie jar.

"Until you left me on the side of the road," Murray said, like he was remembering the jerkoff cop spinning him around, slapping on the bracelets.

Tiras grinned at Rudy. "Whoops." Then, to Murray. "So, man, how long you been out?"

"Couple days."

Tiras arched his eyebrows. What the hell was this honkey doing? Flexin' right out?

"Jack, this is Tiras Williams," Rudy said. "My new partner." Trying to draw the line.

"Good to meet you, Tiras," Murray said, hand outstretched.

Lil' Man jumped in. "You call him Ty, white boy. This ain't no half-ass brother running dope for the man. You best ask somebody."

Murray watched Tiras hold up his hand to Lil' Man as if to hold him off. "And you are?"

"Don't worry about my name, fuckin' cracker."

"What my man's trying to say is that nobody calls me Tiras. Ty makes me sound more respectable. Man's just a little rough around the edges, that's all."

Murray nodded.

"So, Rudy say y'all used to work together."

"Last job we did, things go south. We're outrunning a couple of jumpouts. Rudy takes off in the getaway," Murray splayed his arms out, "leaving me to deal with the mess."

"Screwed up, man."

Murray shrugged.

"So, whatcha want with him now?"

"I was just dropping by."

"Dropping by, huh?" It sounded innocuous enough but not to Murray. "How about we drop by outside?"

"That's all right," Murray said. Then, to Rudy. "I'll be in touch."

Watching Murray walk off, Tiras Williams felt safe enough, and pissed enough, to get in Rudy's face.

"Time to come clean, bitch."

Chapter Four

Rudy's first thought: They were going to kill him. He didn't have a good feeling about it, getting in the back seat while Tiras rode shotgun, Lil' Man driving them out to . . . somewhere. Out to the swamp so they could dump his body.

But that's not what happened.

Right now, Rudy didn't know where they were going, just that Lil' Man was moving Tiras's Escalade—black, polished chrome, with spinners—off the Julia Tuttle and onto 2nd, not sure what good he would be if Tiras was pissed about the whole Jack Murray thing.

He watched from the backseat as Lil' Man and Tiras went back and forth, bullshitting, but not really paying enough attention to tell what they were saying, not bothering to decipher their language.

When they turned into Lincoln Fields, Rudy popped up, eyes looking out the window in all directions. "You mind telling me where we're going?"

It was the first time Tiras had turned around since they got in the car twenty minutes ago. "We going pick up Kwame," he said, turning around, matter-of-fact like it was some routine, something Rudy should have known was happening.

Rudy just said, "Oh," and sat back, wondering if he missed something. He let it go for a couple of blocks before saying, "For what?" Tiras didn't break from his conversation, Rudy thinking he didn't say it loud enough. He said it again, raising his voice. Tiras's mouth stopped moving and everything got quiet, just the rap music from the radio making noise. Rudy caught Lil' Man's eyes in the rearview, then watched them get smaller and the skin wrinkle when he could tell Lil' Man was grinning at him.

Tiras stared at him. Hard. Not saying anything, just turned around in his seat, big white eyeballs giving him a look like, *Watch yourself.*

Rudy said it again, this time in a tone almost apologetic, like he raised his voice just to get their attention and now he was going to spring his real question on them.

Tiras turned back, facing straight ahead, Lil' Man glancing at Rudy in the rearview, grinning still. Tiras let a second pass before he said, "For something I need to get done."

Tiras told Lil' Man to slow down, that they were coming up to the end of the block, then to hang a left. "Go ahead and creep," meaning for Lil' Man to roll slowly by the block so he could find the house. Rudy could see Tiras looking, trying to find the house number, then using his finger to count off the houses as they went by. Tiras put his hand on Lil' Man's arm when he saw a shadow standing on one of the front porches. "Hold up, this is it."

Kwame came in on the driver's side, pushing Rudy over as he got in, a duffel bag taking the spot between them.

Tiras slapped Kwame on the knee, giving him a loud "Kwam' dog," as he took his hand away, then turned partway in his seat. "Wassup, nigga?"

Kwame shook his head, tilting it, then his body. "Wassup-wassup."

Tiras gave him a wide smile, nodding his head, saying, "Not too damn much, nigga," like they hadn't seen each other for a while and now there was some new recognition there. He tapped Lil' Man on the shoulder and pointed out, ready to move away from the curb. Tiras turned the volume up, bouncing to the thump of the rhythm. Over the music, he said, "You ready to do this shit?"

Rudy couldn't hear himself, and he didn't really want to talk anyway, so he just thought about it.

Do what?

Tiras stayed turned towards the backseat, pulling at the handles of Kwame's duffel bag. "What you got in there, man?"

Rudy was talking to himself while Tiras listened to Kwame talk about what was in the bag, watching him take out each weapon right after talking about it. Rudy watched; watched Kwame pass a nine-millimeter and a sawed-off shotgun to the front seat; watched Kwame sift through a couple of hunting knives in there, Kwame pulling one out, jeez, a big one, and hold it up in the light coming through the front windshield, turning it this way and that, enjoying it; watched Lil' Man reach for the three-pound sledgehammer, whacking it in mid air to see how it would feel.

Sledgehammer?

Christ.

The first thing Rudy thought about doing, considering they were still going slow enough, was jump out of the car. Get up and run, man, just run like a wild man, jumping fences in backyards until he got to the next cross street. Cross that one and keep doing the same thing until he couldn't anymore. More than likely he would've lost them. Instead, he was trying to get answers from a man with a sawed-off shotgun on one arm and a roach clip at his lips. It was over now, Rudy knew, with Tiras hitting the chronic. Like talking to a wall.

He gave it a try anyway.

"What's all this for?"

Tiras didn't say anything at first, just brought the roach back up to his lips and sucked in. He let it out, let the cough pass so his voice could calm when he said, "Kwame."

Kwame grunted, choking down his own smoke, nodding to Tiras, who said, "Rudy here want to know what all this is for."

They laughed at it, Tiras laughing between inhaling, Kwame coming down off his last hit, laughing clearly. Rudy put his elbow in the passenger door armrest, then rested his chin on his open hand, staring out of the window at what looked like an elementary school with, jeez, barbed razor wire around the playground, having enough of their little game. Rudy thought that maybe he did miss something—which he figured wouldn't be hard considering he didn't even know what language they were speaking most of the time—but didn't really care anymore.

By the time everything cooled down, with Tiras waving, signaling for Kwame to calm himself, Tiras had readied himself to say, "You quit looking out the window, mopin', and pay attention, then you know what's going on. But, I know you can't do that on account of you been moody like a little bitch since you ran into your boyfriend earlier."

There it was. Rudy wanted to call him on it, tell him that whatever was between him and Murray was over a long time ago but had second thoughts. Guy was wound up. He had his posse, and they were hyped, already had his sawed-off, and he was high on grass. What was the point?

"Lemme spell it out for you, man, because obviously you clueless, man . . . fucking lost. This here," Tiras said, bracing the short sawed-off barrel in that monster hand, "for your man Jack Murray."

Rudy said, "What?" Trying to sound like he didn't know what was going on mainly to keep his own ass out of it. "Why, man?" Exasperated.

Tiras said, " 'Cause," like he was laying down the law and that's all there was to that. " 'Cause," the ego not letting him stop, "he poking his nose in business that don't concern him.

You belong to me now," the tone sounding like Tiras was still trying to figure out if he was being disrespected, "not to him." He paused, giving it time to sink in. "Now, you want to tell me where he stay at?"

There was no reasoning with this guy, in his shiny suit with the vest underneath—but no t-shirt like Deion Sanders from fifteen years back—complete with the doo-rag, staring. Waiting. Expecting.

Rudy acted surprised, a *What me?* look coming over his face when he said, "I don't know."

Tiras blanched, smacking his lips, looking out of the front window, showing the frustration, putting on a show for Rudy that was supposed to mean, *I'm doing you a favor by calming the fuck down, man.*

Eyes straight ahead, Tiras said, "You pushing me now."

Rudy took his time, wanting Tiras to stew a little, figuring that he might chill if he thought Rudy was really trying.

"But, I know someone who might."

Tommy Smalls answered the door, boxer shorts with the fly partially open, his paunch sagging out from under the bottom of his wife-beater, saying, "What the fuck do you want?" before even opening the door.

"Rudy?"

As he said it, two black dudes appeared in the doorframe, each coming from an opposite side, one from Rudy's right and the other from his left.

They were inching in front of Rudy now, deadpan stares from one, black sunglasses on the other; the one with the doo-rag and the flashy suit covering anything he might be carrying. The other one was wearing a tank top just like Tommy, except that it was a lot tighter on him and longer. Long enough so that it could hang over his waistband, covering the piece Tommy could tell was tucked in the front of his camouflage pants.

Tommy stood there, boxers sagging, belly hanging out under his tank top, a bowl of Froot Loops in one hand when the one in the flashy suit said, "Where the fuck Jack Murray stay at?"

Tommy didn't back down. But, he didn't move to get in the man's face, either. He said, "Who the fuck are you?" as Tiras passed him, Tiras then circling as soon as he squeezed past Tommy and the doorframe.

Tommy didn't see it, but Kwame had moved into the doorframe by now, racking the slide on that nine-millimeter that was tucked in his pants. "You heard the man."

Tommy didn't answer. He looked first at Kwame, the sound of the slide getting his attention, then, to Tiras, befuddlement coming over his face at that point, then, to Rudy, pissed off at that little bastard for bringing this shit to his doorstep.

Just in case he didn't hear, Kwame cocked the hammer on his pistol. Tommy looked over to Tiras, who he guessed was the head man, to see him leaning forward, eyebrows raised waiting for his answer.

"The Casita," Tommy said. "Near Fourteenth and Collins, right of the gas station if you're looking at it." He paused. "Number two-oh-six."

Tommy waited, thinking maybe the man in the flashy suit was going to say something. When he didn't, it made an awkward silence, making Tommy nervous.

"Rudy, how you been, man?" It was Tommy's nerves talking, trying to tell himself, *See, you told them what they want to know; you're okay.* All the while, the spoon jangling against his cereal bowl from his shaking hand.

Rudy didn't answer. Didn't even look up at him. Couldn't do that much. Rudy kept quiet, ignoring Tommy's questions; kept his head low until he saw Tiras bring the three-pound sledge out of his pants waistband. That caught Tommy's eye and he turned. But, not fast enough before Tiras brought the hammer down to Tommy's mid section.

Tommy doubled over, the cereal bowl making noise dropping to the floor, Froot Loops and milk all over the place. Tiras took the handle, the wood end, knocking it against Tommy's shin, hitting it three times, taking delight at how Tommy would wince each time.

As soon as Tiras disappeared to the back of the apartment, Kwame shut the door and moved in, kicking Tommy in the stomach twice, then one to the head.

Tiras came back, throwing a pillow at Rudy, Rudy wondering, *What the fuck? You want me to put this under his head, make him more comfortable?*

Tiras had to shove Rudy down, get him on his knees, and tell him to put the pillow over Tommy's face. Rudy did it, looking up with big eyes at Tiras, then back at Tommy, waiting for him to kick. But, he didn't. Just lying there. Weak.

Rudy started to apply pressure, hold the pillow down over Tommy's face when Tiras stopped him. Looking up, Rudy saw Tiras motion to Kwame for that extra nine in his pocket. In one motion, Tiras took the gun from Kwame, put it in Rudy's hand and moved it right up to the pillow, guiding it, stopping when they could feel the outline of Tommy's face.

Rudy looked up again, his face telling Tiras that he didn't want to do this shit.

Kwame put his nine-millimeter on Rudy's head, saying, "You gonna do it or you gonna end up like him."

Rudy turned, hands trembling, unsure of it all, the gun barrel frozen, staying pressed against Tommy Smalls's head through the pillow.

"That's right," Rudy heard Tiras say. "Get it up close."

Murray needed something to calm him down. After all that

atmosphere, he felt wired, not ready for the night to be over. All those women shaking their asses. Then, come home alone. Oh, well. Jerk off then hit the sack. Not before a little winding down time, though. He looked through his CD collection, somewhat limited to begin with but even smaller a year later, sifting through them one by one, flipping each with his index finger. Here we go. George Jones. Nothing like a guy nicknamed "The Possum" to take the edge off. A guy Sinatra called the second best singer ever. Crack open that bottle of Kentucky Gentleman and, man, he could be asleep before he even had a chance to whip his pecker out.

Murray sat back in his chair, his thoughts moving between the dancers but coming back to that one. Miranda. God, she was nice. First thought he had about her was that he wished he would have caught her act.

Jesus, Jack, what's wrong with you? You got a schoolboy crush? Step outside, man, you could maybe score a college chick at The Clevelander, taking in South Beach before but good and liquored up by now. He shrugged it off.

Miranda.

He liked the sound of it. Like it was music. Had somebody ever done a song by that name? If they did, he couldn't recall it right off. He'd like to sing it. Yeah, sing it out like a church choir if that time ever came. Then, he could wake up with her. See that fresh, sort of scrubbed look that he liked about some ladies in the morning. Before all the makeup. Of course, with most of the ladies he'd been with there was a reason for the makeup. But, not her. Thinking about that old Rita Hayworth line, he was pretty darn sure he would go to bed with Gilda and wake up with her, too. Then, she could walk around in her panties and throw on one of his oxfords while they ate breakfast. Still at it, later in the day, Miranda in blue jeans and nice shoes, they could take in a movie.

It was the sound of a car door that got Murray looking out of the window. A black Escalade parked in the alley coming off Collins. The back driver's side door was open but Murray couldn't make the guy out. Big black guy but it was too dark out and there wasn't much light. A few seconds passed before Murray saw the rear passenger side window was down. Murray made out Rudy Maxa in the dome light. And, Tiras Williams in the front, opening the door with one leg hanging out, leaning around the seat, getting after Rudy with his finger in Rudy's face. Then, he saw the one called Lil' Man behind the wheel, stepping out now. Why would he come along? Why not leave the engine running, a guy behind the wheel? They already had a third, the first one out, a guy Murray didn't recognize from earlier. The best Murray could figure, they all wanted to do a tap dance on him.

Just for fun.

The young gal that stuck her head out of 201, ready to bitch somebody out, whoever it was making all that racket with their heavy footsteps, stuck her head back in the room when she saw that black guy coming with a sledgehammer.

They stopped in front of the open doorway to 206. Tiras stepped inside, his back against the door, Beretta nine ready. He motioned for Kwame to move first, next to him against the edge of the door.

Tiras liked how the way they were doing it, like he saw in TV shows, pretty coordinated. There wasn't much to Jack Murray's place—through the living and kitchen area, all one big room, then into the bedroom, where Tiras saw the bed unmade.

"This motherfucker ain't here, man," Tiras said, not sure if anyone was listening.

Lil' Man was in the refrigerator, moving the two-liter Coke bottle out of the way, reaching for orange juice, taking a swig from the carton.

Kwame said, "What you want to do?"

Tiras said, "What *you* want to do?" Then, turning to Lil' Man, "Have dinner, eat the man's food while we wait for him to come back?"

Tiras turned away, looking back at the bed, thinking, *No, doors popped open. That motherfucker saw us. He runnin'.*

Lil' Man replaced the orange juice, closing the refrigerator door when he heard Tiras say, "Shit," turning to see Tiras looking out of a window down to the alley, watching Jack Murray grab Rudy Maxa and run down the alley towards Collins.

Chapter Five

Murray's first instinct was to cross Collins and duck onto Ocean Court, into one of the alleys between buildings. They crossed the street at Collins, a red light giving them the pedestrian walk. Murray noticed the northbound lanes were clear up to Espanola Way, traffic clearing out this time of night on Tuesday.

Murray pulled Rudy Maxa into a taxi turning onto Collins, coming up 14th from Ocean Drive, thanking God for that break. With little traffic going in their direction and the light at Espanola turning green, they could make good time getting away from the Casita. Even better, Murray figured, that Tiras was nose-first in the alley, that they would have to back out onto Collins. Except for a small hiccup in front of The National—beautiful people coming out of stretch limos and foreign sports cars, stopping to pose for cameras—they were crossing 19th in under a minute by Murray's watch.

Murray pulled Rudy Maxa out when the taxi came to a stop in the parking lot next to the Holiday Inn. He wanted to walk, get them away from Collins and off the open parking lot. On the Boardwalk, they stopped in front of Roney Palace. Murray gave a passing glance to two kids making out on the beach. It gave him the couple seconds he was looking for to clear his head, get together the questions he had.

It gave Rudy Maxa some time to deal with his own nerves. He said, "I didn't have anything to do with that," wondering how it sounded coming out. "I didn't know until a few minutes before." Helpless. Yeah, exactly what he was.

Murray said, "Then who did know about it?" Getting to it right away. Following it up, before Rudy could answer, with, "And, why were they there in the first place?"

Rudy said he didn't know, with an "Honest" to punctuate it. It was awkward the way they were standing, both of them facing the beach, maybe trying to look natural, not like there was anything wrong, even if there were only a couple of people around. "That's stuff's screwed up, man." Pause. "I mean, who does that kind of shit?" Rudy turned his body enough to look at Jack Murray. "You know?" With a straight face.

Murray stood there, trying to look relaxed, with a blank expression. *Your friends do that kind of shit, Rudy.*

Murray said, "So, you don't know anything about this?"

Rudy turned to Murray, the stiff tone in his voice inconsistent with that blank expression, saying, "I don't know why he decided to go to your house in the middle of the night or what he's pissed about. With Tiras, it could be anything. Guy's got a short fuse."

Murray could see Rudy start to speak, his hands coming up, starting his shoulder shrug, launching into his Who me? defense. Before he could get it going full bore, Murray said, "I'm standing here, replaying the events in my head, and the first question that comes to mind is, how did they know where I live? How'd you find me?"

"Tommy told him."

"Tommy Smalls?"

Rudy nodded.

Murray grabbed Rudy by the arm, jerking him into a patch of light on the boardwalk coming off the Roney Palace deck.

"That his blood on your shirt?"

Rudy nodded, looking down at the splatter, here and there, tiny bits of it, pinhead-size, across the chest.

My Own Worst Enemy

"What happened?"

"Tiras shot him."

Murray didn't say anything, his face still deadpan, getting close to Rudy's face now. Rudy turned his head and was looking at the two kids still out on the beach, necking before, hormones taking over now, trying to do it in public.

Murray said, "You brought them to Tommy?"

"Guys were hopped up, passing guns around. One guy had a sledgehammer, for chrissakes," Rudy said, nerves coming and going in his voice. "What would you do?"

Again, Murray didn't say anything. He could tell Rudy that he wouldn't have to make that decision, that he wouldn't run with a bunch of gangbangers. He'd been doing what he's doing for as long as he cared to remember, and he couldn't think of one time, not ever, going to some guy's house in the middle of the night with a sledgehammer.

But, that would start a whole thing Murray wasn't interested in getting into.

Instead, he said, "Where's the take from the Coral Gables job?"

"Gone."

Rudy was getting used to Murray not saying anything, like he was now. It was weird—a sense of calm that he could tell his story without fear of Murray blowing up. He said, "I got out quick, man, quick as I could. I didn't know what you were gonna do."

"You mean like naming you as my co-conspirator? That's what they called you in court. My co-conspirator."

"Jesus, they make it sound so criminal."

"It is."

Before Rudy could start, Murray said, "Where'd you go?"

"Bahamas."

Murray thought about it. Him, fighting off that two-hundred-fifty pound Aryan fucker the night of December 5—two weeks after he had arrived at Okeechobee. Putting his weight into a solid uppercut at the guy's breastbone when the asshole bent down to touch his dong. Rudy, relaxing on a beach with a pina colada.

Rudy said, "I spent a few weeks there, in Freeport. Got hot at the craps table at the Isle of Capri Casino. Ran it up to seventy grand and some change."

"What happened after that?"

"Came back for my girl."

"Faye? Why not just call her, tell her to come out?"

"Well," Rudy took a couple of seconds, "I was with another chick at the time."

"Homesick?" Murray said, waiting for Rudy to say something. When he didn't, Murray said, "So, what happened to the money? You end up losing it?"

"Tiras has it."

Murray was losing his blank expression, feeling that he was getting royally screwed in all of this. He calmed himself before saying, "How'd that happen?"

"It's a long story."

"We're doing good so far. You don't have anything else to do."

Rudy slumped.

He said, "I'm getting high at a friend's house, chillin' out. His roommate used to get junk from Tiras. Anyway, this guy . . ."

"The roommate?"

Rudy nodded, then, "This guy starts getting it somewhere else. He was one of Tiras's regulars. Guy always had tons of shit, so it cut into Tiras's profit when he wasn't coming to him anymore. Anyway, he shows up at the house, starts shooting up the place. I tell him I'll give him anything if he lets me live."

"And, you tell him you had this money stashed away?"

"I got nervous."

Murray sort of liked it, asking questions like a cop would. It's the first time he could remember he ever asked this many questions of somebody, feeling like he was an investigator, fishing for the truth.

Maybe he would have made a good cop.

"Rudy, you're making me curious." Even sounding like a cop now. "Tiras has the money," he said. "Why are you still alive?"

Rudy said, "Kept me in a house, I don't know whose, three days. In case they thought I was going to go to the police, I guess. Beat the crap out of me, too. At least once a day. I had already told him I had a way for him to make some big money, but I guess he wanted to see if I was for real."

"On top of the seventy thousand?"

This was news to Murray.

Murray said, "What's this other deal? The one you told Tiras about?"

"After I got back, I went up to Atlanta, see a guy I used to work for lives up there now, guy named Lloyd Bone. Badass sounding name, but real nice guy. I try to keep in touch with him when I can."

When he can. When he's not too busy.

"We're catching up on old times, sitting around drinking bourbon and I tell him about my past few days . . ."

"You tell a guy named Lloyd Bone you have seventy thousand dollars, what, in the trunk of your car? Parked outside?"

"You have to understand this guy. He's old school, got scruples. Not like the maniacs I'm dealing with now."

Murray shrugged, making like he understood.

"He's totally cool with it. Even congratulates me, like he's happy to see something good happen to me."

"You tell him how you got away?"

Rudy thought about it for a second. "I must've forgot about

it at that moment. Anyway, he tells me about some stuff he's into. Mainly scag. But, he mentions he's got a new hookup for machine guns. He starts naming them off . . . AK-47s, TEC-9s, MP-5s, some stuff I never even heard of. Says he makes ten times more off of that than from drugs. Then, he says I can get into that, quote, 'Anytime I want,' " Rudy explained, impressed with himself.

Murray said, "So you gave this up to Tiras?"

Rudy nodded.

"They were going to kill me. I had to do something."

"They might still."

"Yeah, well, Tiras is hot for this, so he keeps me close. Has his eye on those TEC-9s. He wants to go into business with Lloyd for himself. But, he can't keep his eye on me forever."

Murray nodded. "You set this up yet?"

Rudy shook his head.

"I'm supposed to give Lloyd a call in a couple days," he said. "I'm sure with Tiras standing right there."

Murray nodded, looking away, showing that he didn't really care about that part.

He said, "You better get going then."

Rudy thought about boosting something to get him back to Liberty City, having his eye on a Taurus, one of the last in the lot next to the Holiday Inn. It was old enough where anyone who happened to be passing by wouldn't pay attention. But, then the hassle of losing it somewhere along the way, not too close to home. Even if he left it someplace open and the police found it and dusted it, he'd never had a hit for grand theft and you needed three in Florida before you went down and even then it wasn't a sure thing. Probably wouldn't even make it to court.

It was a good bet, but, instead, Rudy handed the cabbie

twenty-something dollars he didn't have to give away as it pulled up in front of his house, not noticing the black Escalade across the street until the taxi moved away from him.

He heard the hiss of the automatic window come down and then made Tiras out in the backseat, motioning for him to come over.

"C'mon, take a ride," Tiras said.

Rudy didn't move. He didn't freeze, but he was sure they knew he didn't want to go. In that second, he could see it playing out: Him saying, *No thanks, I'm tired. It's late.* Trying to play it off. Like there was nothing to talk about. Tiras being polite, asking again, but it sounding more like he was telling Rudy they *were* going for a ride.

Whether he wanted to or not.

Hey, he hadn't called Lloyd Bone yet. So, he was probably safe. Plus, there was no arguing with this guy.

Why not?

Tiras: Where you been?
    Rudy: Nowhere.
    Tiras: Nowhere?
    Pause.
    Tiras: Buuullshit, motherfucker.
    Pause.
    Tiras: One of two things happened tonight. One, that Jack Murray grabbed you while your dumbass wasn't looking. Two, you took off with him hoping you'd never see us again.
    Rudy: He had a gun on me. I had to go.
    Pause.
    Tiras, putting his hand on Rudy's shoulder: I'm gonna need to know what you told him.
    That was how Rudy remembered their conversation before he blacked out. That was the last thing he could recall hearing

Tiras say before he woke up tied to a chair, noticing fresh blood on his shirt. Not Tommy Smalls's blood. That was dried by now.

His own.

Rudy tasted that sour, bitter taste with his tongue, wiping it across the corner of his mouth before he picked his head up. Kwame was standing over him. Grabbing his knuckles.

It was just like the old days. When Tiras first took hold of Rudy, using him for practice. But, that was because . . . they were bored. This was for something else.

Rudy could see them moving. He could make out Kwame moving back and forth, rubbing his knuckles, then fading to a blur as he cocked back and faked coming at him again with his right cross. Tiras was a blur, too, Rudy able to make him out sitting on a chair across the room, raising his hand at Kwame, saying, "Don't let him bleed on my carpet."

The first thing Rudy heard Tiras say when he came into focus was, "I don't want to do this, Rudy."

Tiras waited for Rudy to answer. When he didn't, Tiras kept going.

"I want this to be simple," he said. Calm. "This nigga right here," pointing to Kwame, "loves this shit. He can do this all night." Meaning they weren't having a discussion. "Personally, I don't want you bleedin' all over my things."

Rudy took a minute, partly to make Tiras wait, mostly to gather himself, before he said, "He had a gun. I told you."

Tiras walked over to Rudy, putting his hand on Rudy's cheek to move his head at an angle where he could look at Rudy's cut lip in the light. Examining him. Like a concerned doctor.

Rudy heard Tiras tell him that it was pretty bad, that he should have it looked at, realizing that it was all for show.

Tiras took his hand away from Rudy's face, letting it come back upright before putting his face close to Rudy's. "I'm going

My Own Worst Enemy

to be your friend now," he said. "But, if I see Jack Murray try to get anywhere near you or my money, this ain't nothing compared to what I'm going do to you."

So much for being a friend.

"Or him."

There she was, Miranda, stepping from the sterile white Corsica, the attendant catcalls coming from the fellas on the steps leading into the office at 16320 Northwest Second Avenue, North Miami Beach. Standing around looking busy.

She liked this skirt, the black Dolce, one from her ex before she found him with his secretary. *How cliché* was the first thing that ran through her mind. *I'm not giving back the nice stuff you gave me* was the next. She never understood why she heard about women that would show up with a box full of things from the relationship. Hey, these are nice things. As for the things you had at my place, check Goodwill.

Miranda tugged at it, wondering if the guys were looking when she stepped out of the car. This was the problem. It was too short.

"Damn, girl, we got to get together," one of them said, smiling at her. She thought his name might have been Pedro. She wasn't sure, but she knew the face. And, the manner. Office playboy-type. Calling her "girl" like there was something familiar there. The most familiar thing to her was that she remembered his b.o.

She was trying to fit a hip holster into the waistband. It was a bit tight, but, dammit, it was going to fit. Adjusting the leather into the crook of her hipbone, she heard Bill Cecil, her supervisor, say, "What's going on?" as he walked through the double doors towards her.

Miranda's gaze moved away from her hip to her boss that she always thought looked like a tractor salesman and said, "I met a guy last night."

"At the club?"

Miranda nodded.

She waited while Bill Cecil reached into his pocket for a notepad, licked his finger before flipping pages, popped his pen cap and said, "What's his name?"

"Jack Murray."

"Jack Murray," Cecil said while writing, slow, like he was trying to search the memory banks to put a face to it. Then, "Nope. Going to have to check him out."

Miranda didn't say anything and surprised herself with the tinge that ran through her after Bill Cecil's words. It was a sense of relief. Glad that her boss had never heard of him.

"That doesn't surprise me," she said, readjusting the fit of her holster. "I've never seen him around, either. He might be new in town or maybe just a face to put as a front. Whoever he is, he must be a good friend of Caesar's because he's the new manager."

Cecil's brow went up. "That's somebody I need to get to know better."

"Me, too."

Cecil frowned. "So, how long you talk to him?"

Miranda was noncommittal. Shrugging, she said, "Five minutes. Maybe. He caught me in the dressing room."

"Caught you? Doing what?"

"Dressing, Bill." Playing the father figure. "He caught me dressing. He knocked on my door, asked if I needed any help getting ready."

"Sounds like a gentleman." Cecil frowned again when he saw Miranda smile. "What else you two talk about?"

She could see him studying her, that look in her face like she was remembering what Jack Murray looked like. He didn't know where to take it from here, and he could tell she wasn't going to help any. Especially after she shrugged at his last question.

"That's it?" Cecil said. "So, what's your impression?"

"About six feet tall, dark hair, brown eyes . . ."

"Outside of that," Cecil said, not looking up from his notepad but not having written anything yet, waiting for her to say something he wanted to hear. "I mean, what's he like. Not what's he *look* like."

"I get the feeling he's not a player like some of the others. Doesn't strike me as it, anyway. Too early to tell, though. He seems too nice."

Cecil said, "Don't get too attached to this guy," still writing. "You don't know anything about him."

She could see his point. But, what was she supposed to do, date one of these cowboys? Women got in their way—until their laundry needed doing. She'd always had something for rogues. Not in the literal sense and not the out-and-out jerks like she worked with, but a Doc Holliday-type that romanced you in his best suit with one eye on your diamond necklace. Or James Mason, with the voice that told you there was danger shrouded just beneath the unassuming veneer. She got that vibe from Jack Murray. As far as she was concerned, there was nothing morally precarious about the fact that she was smitten from afar with him. He was the first man in a long time that didn't make innuendo about going to bed with her. He *listened,* instead of just standing there waiting for his turn to talk. Maybe he did that normally, but he didn't with her.

Looking at Bill Cecil, she continued, "You asked me my impression of him. I'm telling you."

"Miranda, try not to forget one small detail. These guys are gangsters, and you're with the FBI."

Chapter Six

Jack Murray couldn't remember the last time he saw South Beach this early. Ten o'clock. None of the nouveau-bullshit artsy folk—the models, the actors, the fashionable gays—made it out before lunch. Most of what he saw were the tourists and the old Jewish people moved down from New York.

Murray arched himself, hands inverted on the small of his back. There was something else he found himself not able to remember. The last time he hurt this bad. The floor of one of the dressing rooms in his new club was a rough way to spend the night.

It wasn't long before it came to him about the problem in front of him. Before people started asking, "What happened to Tommy Smalls?" Or, "Anybody seen Tommy?" Talk like that. Nip all that in the bud. Before it gets to be a big deal.

Nipping it in the bud meant, of course, going to Caesar about it. Murray figured he should anyway, seeing as Tommy worked for him and word would eventually get back. Better to do it early—and do it himself—than for Caesar to hear it secondhand. But, damnit, this was exactly the kind of thing he wanted to avoid. Getting too involved. He thought of that scene in *Godfather 3*. The one where Pacino says every time he tries to get out, they pull him back in.

Right before he has a stroke.

One of Caesar Pelli's favorite things in the world was hanging out in Bermuda shorts, a short-sleeve guayabera shirt with the collar open, showing his chest hair and gold chain around his neck. Looking the part of a Mafia don. The genuine article, like he was just off the boat from Palermo. Or what he thought they might have looked like in the '50s or '60s.

Easing back into his deck lounger, Caesar thought back to those times. Times when they were the biggest thing going. All the glitz, the glamour. Cache. Some of the guys palling around with JFK, The Rat Pack. Respected men. Men with an aura. A mystique. The South Florida family running around in those guayabera shirts like the one he had on now. With the chinos. Looking the part. You look the part, nobody'll fuck with you. Now, his guys looked, and lived, mostly like lower middle-class. Except for him. But, he was the boss. Made his way up, showed people not to fuck with him and, when the time came, was in the right place at the right time.

He raised his glass, waiting for Gina to fill it. Not saying anything, playing a role.

She came over, filling his tumbler with one-part Coke, two-parts bourbon. Then, taking a washcloth soaked in ice water, she put it on his forehead and listened to him moan. The powerful don moaning like a girl over cold water. Enjoying how cool it was. Cool for him. Shit for her. Putting on this act, so somebody passing by can notice the big shot in slip fifty-eight. What she wanted people to notice—and knew that they were—was her ass in a g-string bikini and her tits hanging out of the top.

What Caesar didn't like were his guys showing up with their ratty jeans and a t-shirt, for chrissakes. One rule of his: If you're going to come in daylight, be dressed for the occasion. Bad for the image otherwise.

Usually he could count on Jack Murray to follow that rule. Not a suit but slacks and a nice shirt. Respectable. But, today . . . It brought Caesar out of his chair, watching Murray walk up to the bow in shorts and a white BVD v-neck. Bags under the eyes.

Wrinkled.

"Jack?" Caesar said. "What the hell happened to you?"

Murray looked past Caesar, watching Gina, though her name didn't come to him right away. When he looked back at Caesar, he could see the expectation on the old man's face, the hands coming up waiting for an answer.

Murray stepped onto the deck. Landing, he said, "Had some trouble last night."

"A customer?"

Murray shook his head. He sat back on the deck sofa, leaning his head back, gathering it up, sighing, before saying, "Tommy Smalls is dead."

Caesar sat upright. Interested now. He had his hand over the rim of his glass as he came up, asking Murray how it happened and if it was some husband or boyfriend Tommy pissed off.

"It had to do with me," Murray said. He waned a bit, wanting to be prodded for the rest of it. It was a long story, some of it he didn't feel like getting into. No real way around it, though. "Some guys were looking for me. They went to Tommy to find out."

"What guys?"

"Involved with Rudy Maxa."

Caesar nodded, telling Murray that he recalled Rudy's name. "Jack, that's not Rudy Maxa's sort of thing." Caesar looked around, gesturing, trying to figure out what to say. "He's too much of a woman. Fragile."

"Yeah, but the guys he runs with now aren't."

"Who we talking about?"

Murray leaned over and rested his elbows on his knees. He said, "Guy named Tiras Williams," with an interested look.

Caesar turned to Gina and told her something that Murray couldn't hear. She disappeared into the main cabin for a moment and came back out, strutting for the good-looking young guy in his swimming trunks—shirt off—following her.

Caesar took a sip. "Never heard of him."

That didn't surprise Murray.

"What is he, black fella?"

Murray nodded.

"Jack," Caesar said when the young guy in his swimming trunks made it over to them, "this is Nicky Silva. I want him to hear this."

Caesar didn't say anything else, like who Nicky was or what he was doing there. But, Murray could figure it out. The guy flexed his bicep shaking Murray's hand. Young guy, coming up the ranks. Hotshot looking to make his mark.

"You see, that's the problem," Caesar said, getting back to the topic. "Twenty years now, you got all these groups moving in. Guatemalans, Argentineans, Columbians. They get off the boat, and they're moving that hard stuff. Jigaboos, too. Crack. Heroin. Kill each other over it." Yeah, while the old bosses were being passed over by sticking to the traditional stuff. "Run around in their fancy clothes and their shiny cars."

Murray glanced around the deck then back at the old man.

Caesar took a sip. "Animals."

Gina moved in over Caesar's shoulder now, massaging him. Murray saw her look over her shoulder at Nicky, who looked back. Murray could tell there was a recognition there. It told him she was stupid. Stupid to be that out of touch with her place here. Caesar would catch her doing that. He could dump her off of Bimini and have ten women, each younger than her, lined up to take her place. And, Nicky, the young stud, riding the wave that came with just being around the boss. Fuck it all up with behavior like that. It had happened before.

"What's this guy's problem?" Caesar said.

Murray shrugged and said, "He's got his hands deep in Rudy's pockets," knowing that it didn't sound like much of a problem to right-thinking people.

But, to that guy.

"And, he figures you're trying to do the same?"

Murray knew Caesar could relate.

Caesar was grinning now, taking it in, shaking his head, thinking about it. "You know where to find this guy?"

Murray shook his head.

"Well, you find out."

Murray wondered how long his front door had been open. It was sometime around two in the morning, maybe later, when he took off, not worrying about locking up on his way out. Ten o'clock when he looked out of the front window of The Platinum Pony, watching tourists and old ladies. Hour-and-a-half, maybe two hours, round trip to see Caesar. Tack on the half-hour trying to find parking for that black Taurus he spotted in the Holiday Inn parking lot last night, partly to see if his skills were still up to snuff. Plus, how else was he going to get to Fort Lauderdale?

Murray sat back on the wicker couch. He looked around at the bare walls, the 13-inch color TV, the wicker bed frame, the wicker armchair. Hell, the wicker end table next to the wicker armchair. Not looking forward to the rest of his day, wondering what he could do to get out of it. Or, put it off. Maybe he should just leave. Go somewhere far away or, at least, as far as the hundred-seventeen dollars in cash he had on him would take him. Someplace exotic.

Like Pensacola.

He could explain it to Caesar, like he tried to before. Just put more behind it this time. Not let himself get sidetracked. Sit him down, he could pretend Caesar was his old man, talk to him like that. Murray put it behind him, stretching out on the couch, checking his watch on the way down. Twelve-forty. Lay down for a few minutes before making some calls. Twelve-forty, huh? He remembered seeing Miranda on the schedule. Working the twelve-to-two. Well, he remembered seeing "Shelly" on the schedule anyway, now pretty sure that that was her. Maybe giving a different name because she didn't want a job as stripper coming back to haunt her when she got a real job. Whatever the case, he was in charge right now and wasn't going to press it.

Thinking back on it, he didn't see a Miranda on the schedule anywhere. And, he would've remembered that name. Different from the Ebony, or the Chastity, or the two Vixens that he did see on the roster. There wasn't another Shelly as far as he knew.

Murray sat up, checking his watch again. Twelve-forty-five.

Yeah, maybe go by. Just to be sure.

After her first set, Miranda got out of her boots. The uncomfortable white leather thigh high zip-up ones. She wondered if Jack Murray would be coming in. Maybe not this early. She told herself to start requesting more night shifts. It was crowded and more of a chance to see him. She told herself what she actually meant was more of a chance to witness the illegal activity that Bill Cecil was certain the club was a front for.

Miranda walked barefoot over to the dressing room door and looked out into the hallway. At the end, near the stage, she saw the back of Jack Murray, talking to the DJ, in a black polo shirt and khakis. Nice butt.

She had one more set to go in her last hour. Then, maybe . . . She double-timed it back to the vanity, wanting to freshen her makeup.

Oh, and find some better shoes.

★ ★ ★ ★ ★

To Murray, Rafael Rojas would always be the guy everyone knew as Chuco: A guy with no other purpose in life other than to get high. As many times a day as he could, as many days of the week as he could, as many weeks of the year as he could. Murray wondered, by now, if Chuco even knew what time of the year it was. Or, what year it was.

He'd be getting high right now, two-thirty in the afternoon. Murray took that in and kind of respected it. Not in anybody's way. Not part of the rat race. Not striving for too much. Kept it simple.

Murray parked the Taurus in the South Pointe Park lot, about the only place he ever saw in South Beach you could just arrive and park. At the end of Washington Avenue, past the intersection with Biscayne Boulevard. Away from all the art deco kitsch and the tourists surrounding Ocean Drive.

For a guy who liked to keep low and who never seemed to have any cash on him, Chuco had a great big monster of a car. A classic, really. 1957 Buick Century. Bright yellow going all the way back to the fins, with a white swath through the middle. White rag top. Murray saw it as he pulled up, noticing how every time he did see it, it looked like it had just been waxed. When he's not smoking dope, maybe he spends his free time waxing his car.

Murray was checking out the saw blade rims, looking through the windows at the upholstery. Pristine. The only thing he thought that maybe wasn't original was the radio. He couldn't make out the brand name, but there wasn't a knob on it. Murray moved a finger along the top of the passenger side door—like he was giving it the white glove test—readying himself for the beach to look for Chuco. Anyone looking for him could just look for that big monster of a car and he was somewhere nearby.

He started that way and saw a pair of eyes looking back at

him, a woman's body turned on its side on the trunk of the car.

"Jack?"

Murray jumped back, not sure at first. Standing there in the sun, he put his hand up to block the light.

"Marisol?"

She nodded, giving Murray a grin when she did it, taking off her sunglasses and relaxing on her hip. "What're you doing here?"

"Looking for him," Murray said, tapping the rear fin. "Where is he?"

Marisol motioned out past the end of the parking lot. "Over there." Rolling her eyes. She looked out towards the boardwalk then the other way to the marina and Biscayne Bay. "I don't know what you want him for. That's all he ever does, gets wasted with his friends."

"He's good for a few things," Murray said, hoping he was right. He could see it now, himself trying to reason with Chuco, hunched down having to take a couple of hits just to get in good graces.

Marisol said, "Well, one of the things he's not good for is getting his little *pepe* hard when he's always on that shit." She turned on her stomach. "And, I was a fluffer, for crying out loud."

Fluffer? Murray thought he was a pretty cool guy, someone who kept up with what was going on, but that was a new one on him. He kept his face deadpan, hoping to play off that he'd never heard it before.

Marisol waited for him to say something, giving Murray a look, trying hard to look natural. "You know, like in the porno movies? A fluffer keeps a guy hard when they're not filming."

Murray looked past that shiny wave of black hair, like the symmetrical waves he saw beyond her moving through Government Cut right now, then back down to her nicely browned ass cheeks.

"Yeah, I spent a couple of years in L.A.," she said. See what he thought about that, sure she had his attention by now. "Kept a guy hard for an hour-and-a-half once."

It actually went through Murray's mind why she would have to do that for so long, seeing as how he didn't figure there to be much production value in pornos. No need for that kind of time between takes. What were they waiting for? The actor to figure out his motivation? Maybe he was wrong but he asked the question, never mind the question he should have asked about why she was doing that job in the first place. Marisol told Murray the girl the guy was working with was stuck in traffic.

"Why get started so soon then?" Murray said. "You probably could've waited."

Marisol was thrown off by the almost-genuine sound in Murray's voice. " 'Cause I wanted to." Trying hard.

Murray nodded, feeling a hand moving up the inseam of his pant leg. "Show must go on, huh?"

Marisol nodded, that little grin still with her. She had her chin cupped in her left hand, her right one feeling up Murray's leg until she felt him move away.

"What's wrong?"

Like they had something.

Murray tried to keep on track, think about what he had to do. "I have to see your boyfriend."

Marisol turned over on her back like it was the time to tan that side. "Last I saw, they were just off the boardwalk," she said, checking a wristwatch laying next to her, steaming over trying to get Jack Murray in the backseat of her boyfriend's car. "You guys have fun together."

Marisol was right. Last she saw, they were right off the boardwalk, and that's where Murray saw Chuco and two others he didn't recognize as he made the top of the walkway leading to the beach. He stopped, leaning against the railing where the walkway met the end of the boardwalk. Murray looked around, back to South Pointe Park, then down the beach then up to the end of the pier and out into the Atlantic. Jesus, could they be more obvious? Not really quiet about it, passing joints around like lollipops. Pretty loud about it, come to think of it.

Murray thought about coming on as some off-duty cop before they had a chance to see him. Walk up behind them and make some stupid joke. It might take too long for Chuco to get the joke, and his boys would look at Murray like he was some kind of asshole. He looked the part, though, in his creased khaki pants and ironed polo shirt and his best pair of loafers, out of place here. As he walked off the steps from the walkway, Murray saw one of Chuco's friends look over at him then away. Like nothing. There went his cop joke. Like they could care less.

Murray stopped still right in front of them, hands on his hips, taking a second to glance at the hazy shoreline, the hotels in a row like some desert mirage.

He could tell they were, well . . . nonplussed. Murray kicked the leg of the one in the middle just to get him to look up.

"What the fuck?" Chuco said, looking up, giving the once-over to the wiry frame in front of him. "Jack Murray."

Murray didn't say anything, just nodded.

Which was just what Chuco remembered he did the first time they met. Six years ago, doing a weekend in the Dade County lockup. Chuco stayed close to Murray, that easygoing nature said he was used to that jail environment. That county time was bush league stuff. Chuco thought, *For me, man, that's hard time. I can't be in here with all these ass fuckers, man.*

Murray was on his haunches, ignoring Chuco introducing him to the hopheads on either side of him. "Chuco, you remember Rudy Maxa?"

Getting right to it.

Chuco took a hit and nodded while he held it.

"You know where I can find him?"

Chuco took a hit and shook his head while he held it.

Jeez, like talking to a two-year-old.

Murray grabbed the joint, trying to get this guy to focus. He asked again about where Rudy Maxa might be, knowing that he wasn't in the same place as eighteen months ago when Murray went away.

Chuco took some time, trying to help his good friend Jack Murray out with all these questions. He said, yeah, snapping his fingers, that he had a job about six months ago. Down in Homestead. "I needed a good safe man. I called over there a few times. Even went over there once. His old lady's there, but she's always pissed off 'cause he's never around. After a couple days of that, I gave up. She was depressing me. All that bitching."

"Who's the woman? Faye? They still together?"

Chuco nodded. "Yeah, must've been her. Don't recall the name, but they been together long as I known him, so if you ask they still together, I figure it's the same one."

"You remember where she lives?"

Man, that Jack Murray sure has a lot of questions. Chuco watched the joint in Murray's hand, him holding clinched between his middle finger and thumb. "Over in Liberty City. Ten-eighty Northwest Sixty-ninth. I remember that because it's my birthday. October, nineteen-eighty."

Murray fake-smiled, surprised Chuco remembered his birthday. Or, that October was the tenth month. Thankful that he could in this case. He tossed the joint in Chuco's lap and watched him take a quick drag before doing anything else.

"I help you, Jack?" The words coming out between breaths.

Murray waved at the smoke, saying, "I never had it so good."

Chuco smiled, took another hit and asked Murray if he wanted some. Shit, yeah, you could hang out, take a load off. We could catch up.

"Nah," Murray said. "I got some place to be."

Chapter Seven

They met at the Fairchild Tropical Gardens. It was Miranda's idea—to meet somewhere in public, sit in the sun so she could wear her favorite skirt, be around families. It wasn't the short one that her ex gave her. That wouldn't go with the whole family thing. Plus, she didn't want the stench of that relationship here. Start fresh. With a tan Dolce and Gabbana pencil skirt her mom bought her because she thought Miranda needed to start dating again.

She knew Murray wouldn't be scared by the family scene; she knew he could tell that she didn't want that. She just wanted to get away from the club and feel comfortable with him.

They started with the guided walking tour. Probably the last of the day seeing as how it was nearing three-thirty. They passed the Richard Simmons rainforest. Murray thought it was weird that they would name a rainforest for an exercise guy. Couldn't have been the same guy, right? But, he didn't know any other Richard Simmonses. Maybe it was a bigwig in the rainforest world. He thought about making a joke about it but couldn't find the right delivery on the spot like that. It could fall flat. Ruin the impression he was trying to make.

He let it go.

They sat under a tree, something by the best Murray could make out from the brochure was called *Vitex agnus-castus*. He looked under the column that said "common name." The Chaste tree. Hmm.

Sunlight knifed through the branches, Miranda liking how the shade cut across Murray's midsection, accentuating certain parts of him like the body that was toned not like he was in any real shape but had been in construction or worked with his hands all his life. Murray liked the way the shade stopped at Miranda's hips, leaving her legs in the sun.

Miranda started talking to him about movies. It was an easy way to lean into conversation with him, something just about anybody could relate to. Anything to stay away from club talk. The both loved Steve McQueen. They had decided that *Bullitt* was both of their favorites. Best thing about that one, Murray said, was Norman Fell. "Yeah, Mister Roper giving old Stevie-boy the riot act, calling him 'a sick.' "

Miranda thought it was cute, Jack Murray starting to feel loose. Talkative. She was quiet.

"*Great Escape* was kickass, too," he said. Murray couldn't buy that she liked McQueen in his Navy dungarees in *The Sand Pebbles*. Murray said that his cousin used to be in the Navy and all the stories he had about the insecure, immature assholes ordering people around like they've actually earned respect sounded like too much bullshit. So, he was never inclined to like any military movie very much.

On *The Thomas Crown Affair:* She liked the remake. "They didn't stay faithful to the original." Murray said it like that was the bright line for a good remake. "I guess two million dollars just doesn't carry the weight it used to." She watched Murray pick a few blades of grass, wondering about what to say next. Which was, "Thing I never got about that one, how're they going to send a girl in, expecting her to catch Steve McQueen?"

She asked him about music. "I don't think most people ever heard of most of the music I like," Murray said. Lalo Schifrin or John Coltrane were probably his favorites. He made it a point to say that they were household names, but he'd bet anyone that if Gallup took a poll more than half the country wouldn't know who they were. He knew this after bouncing around the tube one day, stopping on MTV and watching some redhead asking Bill Clinton who his favorite performer was and him replying "Thelonius Monk."

"This chick comes back and asks the man who was about to be president—" Murray slowed down for effect "—who 'the loneliest monk' was. Unbelievable." Murray smiled to himself, trying to gauge if Miranda thought it was as ridiculous as he did. "Makes me almost glad I spent time in the hole, away from the world."

Damn. Miranda didn't want to, but it was too hard to resist. Hey, he brought it up. She had pretended to be surprised by the backstage rumors, but wanted to hear his story. He didn't have a prior federal history. She had checked. She rehearsed it before today but still felt her lips mouthing, "So, what'd you do to get thrown in the shithouse?" Not passing judgment, but strong enough to let him know she was laying the groundwork if this was going to have any chance. Miranda was still going over it, staring, when Jack asked her if everything was okay. She wondered if she could make it come out without sounding too harsh. Couch it like she understood.

Miranda saw it playing out: *Sure, everything's okay. I like you a lot. You're an ex-con that'll probably end up getting sucked back in because you don't have any alternative, and I'm an undercover FBI agent that's helping to bust everyone around you, and I pray you don't get in the way. Why would something be wrong?*

Miranda knew she was giving too much time to convince Jack that everything actually was okay when, "Jack, how long were you in jail?" came out.

Murray breathed, scared about getting into this. He said, "One year and one day."

Miranda nodded. "How come?"

Looking and sounding interested.

Murray shook his head, giving Miranda a look like, *Do you really want to do this?* "For associating with people that I had no business associating with."

"Did it involve Caesar?"

Again, Murray shook his head. "Nope."

Good.

"So, you haven't always worked for him?" Miranda asked.

"Nah, I've been working on and off for him since I was eighteen, I guess. He picked me up after my old man passed, but never really made me do anything I didn't want to do. Even this—" Miranda knew Jack meant the club work "—is gravy. I told him I didn't want anything illegal, so here I am."

Great. This was going better than expected. "Nothing illegal." Miranda had faith in her instinct, starting to believe she actually could keep him out of the way. She wanted to ask Jack if he had ever hurt anybody or if that's what he just got out of corrections for, but didn't want to push much further. She didn't read him as a gang-banger—or else she wouldn't be here—and handling herself alone was not a problem.

Murray said, "What about you?" The change was sudden, but not antagonistic.

Most of the time, Miranda would've thought a quick change of topic like that would signal that the guy was a dog and she was digging too close. Her light bulb would go off—bing!—and she'd keep grilling the guy, find out that he saw a different woman that afternoon, et cetera, finagled a free meal out of it, then call it a night. But, she was warming up to Murray. He had withstood a probe about topics much more personal than she was accustomed to giving.

"I was going to school. Central Florida." She hated giving him the cover story. "Wasn't motivated, though. Had a girlfriend down here. Had some part-time jobs here and there, but the money in this is good. I don't know, though . . ."

"It's not the sort of thing you can do forever," Jack interrupted.

"Yeah, but I really don't know what else I'm going to do."

"Neither do I." Murray shrugged. "The only thing I do know is that I don't want to go back to jail."

They laughed together.

Murray walked Miranda back to her car, a nice little red Honda that looked new. Murray thought she must be doing okay at the club. Maybe working too many night shifts with the big tippers. Maybe they liked her too much. Maybe he'd have to start making sure to schedule her more early shifts.

They were both parked way the hell out there, past tourist buses filling up with seniors and people interested in flora and fauna. Past moms and dads boring their kids with a day of looking at trees. In the boonies because they didn't get there until just after three o'clock.

He gave her a peck on the cheek. She thought it was nice. She thought the whole thing was nice.

Miranda had one leg in, leaving the car door open so she could stand and watch Murray as he put keys into the door lock of his black Taurus a couple of aisles over. He caught her looking and gave her a smile as he ducked in. She followed him out of the lot, not on purpose. That's just the way it happened. Sometimes there would be a car between them, sometimes not.

The line of cars scattered when they got off Old Cutler Road, most everyone taking the roundabout to get onto LeJeune Road. Traffic fanned out when everyone came to Dixie Highway. She was still in back of Murray. Just now there were a few cars that would come in and out between them. She still had her eye on the black Taurus when she was about to make a left turn off onto Southwest 27th Avenue for her apartment.

Miranda thought about it for a minute, coming up on the light for her turn. She figured he would be on his way to work. That's why he didn't ask you for dinner.

Maybe just follow. Make sure he gets there okay.

Murray was pretty proud of himself. Satisfied that he had made a good impression. He was relaxed, put on an air of confidence. It was out of sorts for him, acting like that. Jesus, when's the last time he was on an actual date? An actual *date* date, not taking some chick to the local hangout where his boys were with their chicks, then going home to bang her?

He fumbled with the radio, looking for something to keep the good feelings going. Something to play in the background while he thought of Miranda in different scenes that he could play out in his head. Something he liked to do.

None of the pre-set stations were any good. Mostly country and western. Not that it didn't agree with him, just that it wasn't right for now. Mood music. That's what he wanted. Murray pressed the seek button until he came to a favorite from his old days.

Dr. John. "Right Place, Wrong Time."

That would do.

Well, he sure as hell wasn't going to work.

Miranda followed Murray up Dixie Highway, at first wondering if it wouldn't have been easier for him to get onto Brickell Avenue and take the Venentian across. Then, when she saw him get on I-95. Well, he must plan on taking the MacArthur Causeway.

When he didn't take that . . .

Miranda stayed behind him on 95, traffic moving a steady seventy-miles-an-hour this time of early evening. She had Murray in the center lane, two cars up, then moving into the right lane. He stayed there, except to pass twice.

Miranda tapped her fingers on the steering wheel, turning up the radio. "Right Place, Wrong Time." Good one to get pissed off to.

She followed him off the exit at Northwest Sixty-second Street, pulling up right behind him at the underpass. She kept a couple car lengths behind, letting a Caddy in to give some cover. They were going east on Northwest Sixty-second when she saw Murray hang a left at Northwest Fourth Avenue.

The house Murray stopped in front of was in the second block off Northwest Fourth, right at the intersection with Northwest Sixty-third Street. It looked just like the others, all of them shotgun homes, sometimes a waist-high hurricane fence separating what passed for a yard, paint peeling, Miranda doubting if they cared really.

She did a u-turn before going too far, pretty sure Murray could make her car out now. Nothing else around. She stopped at the sign and watched Murray walk up the porch steps in her rearview mirror.

Well, it wasn't like he lived here. Why wouldn't he pull in if he lived here? No need to park on the street, walk up to the front door sort of apprehensive like he wasn't sure if he had the right house. Like he was doing now.

Okay, so if he didn't live here, who did?

And, is she pretty?

Chapter Eight

It was eight the next morning when Miranda got the call from Natalie Solis, a legal secretary with the Dade County public defender's office that she had met two years ago when Natalie had questions about joining the Bureau. "Yes, Ten-eighty Northwest Fourth Avenue . . . And, that's the name of the owner? . . . And it's rented in his name? . . . M-A-X-A . . . Yeah, let's have lunch sometime this week . . . I'd love to, but I have somewhere to be today . . . Bye."

Miranda was about to get up, grabbing her purse and holster when Harvey Turner, her immediate supervisor, came in and asked her how she was doing. The Harvey Turner that was a federal agent but looked like a stockbroker, the Harvey Turner that headed the Narcotics Task Force trying to bust Caesar Pelli, the same Harvey Turner that convinced Bill Cecil to go to the higher-ups with the fact that Caesar Pelli represented the last of the old guard Mafioso types in South Florida, that he was a threat and that taking his organization down would make for good Bureau public relations, the same Harvey Turner that was the youngest Special Agent-in-Charge in the history of the Miami office and was looking for more.

"Harvey, I was just on my way out," Miranda said, cinching her holster on her skirt.

"Yeah, where to?"

Miranda didn't say anything, just sat down, wanting to leave out the fact that she was acting on information on a private citizen without probable cause. Which is why she called in a favor from a friend with the locals instead of going through her people.

Harvey let it go and sat in the chair across from Miranda's desk. "I wanted to get a sense of where we are in the investigation."

"You didn't talk to Bill? Or, read my reports?"

"I have talked to Bill. And, I've read your initial report and all the updates. There are some things I'd like to hear from you, though, Miranda," Harvey said. "You've been working at the club for almost six months now . . ." He stopped to see if she would try to react to what she thought was coming out of his mouth next. "And, I just want to make sure the Bureau's not financing some moonlighting work so you can get big tips from hard-up conventioneers."

"I just think of that as hazard pay."

Motherfucker.

"Shit, girl," Harvey said, smiling at her, "I like the way you think." Calling her 'girl', getting chummy. "I bet you get good ones, too. Sliding up and down, shaking it up there." The stockbroker trying to sound like he was down with it. "I'd give you a nice big one, too, I was ever in a place like that."

Miranda was quiet. Her gaze moved from the stockbroker's face smiling at her to his wedding ring, then back.

Harvey's smile went away.

"All joking aside," he said.

She didn't find any of it particularly funny.

"You've been in there quite a while now, and I just had some questions."

Miranda started to speak, trying to head it off, tell the man everything was in her reports. He put his hand up, looking down at her reports in his lap, without looking up at her.

"Your report of May fifteen, you say there was someone who

dropped off a bag . . ."

"A duffel bag," Miranda said.

"Yeah, a duffel bag," Harvey said, slow like he was re-reading it, "at the dj booth. A few hours later, Caesar himself came in and picked it up." He licked his thumb and flipped a page in the manila folder with the clasps at the top. "And, it happened again in your report of June ten."

"That's what it says."

Harvey flipped a couple more pages. "Doesn't mention it happening again."

Miranda leaned back in her chair, the look on Harvey's face telling her he wasn't sure where he was going with it. And, she wasn't in a hurry to help him along.

"That's good," Harvey said, the stockbroker trying to sound excited. "That might be a drop. No telling what sort of illegal contraband is in there. We can use that in an affidavit if we go forward."

"What do you mean 'if'?"

Again, Turner held a hand up without looking at Miranda. "Your last report makes mention of a new manager . . ."

"Jack Murray."

That got him looking up. "So, you met him?"

"Of course I did," she said. "He's my boss."

She knew that stung him, the stockbroker always making it a point to tell her *he* was her boss.

Harvey said, "You seem to be getting confused."

Knowing what he meant.

"You talk to him at all?"

Miranda nodded her head. "Yeah, we talked about different things," she said, careful not to give too much away. "All he did was, really, was introduce himself."

"That's it, introduce himself?"

Again, she nodded. "There's a lot of girls working there. He wouldn't have the time to carry on a conversation with all of them. And, I don't even think he wants to," she said, telling herself that. "I saw him one more time, yesterday, but we didn't talk."

Harvey nodded, the crook in his mouth telling Miranda he was taking it in.

"Harv . . ."

"Harvey."

"Harvey, what exactly do you think I'm doing here? Enjoying this? That I like having degenerates hootin' and hollerin' at me, practically naked up there?"

He hesitated. "Miranda, I don't know what you're doing or how you feel about it. That's why I'm here, talking to you."

"You ever work undercover? Play a role, try like hell to get them to like you, confide in you—but not too much—so that they think exactly what you want them to think?"

Harvey shook his head, teeth clinched, lips tight, with the jawbone twitching.

"No? You came up so fast you never had that opportunity. Never had to be out in that position."

"Miranda, I don't have to explain myself to you, or prove myself, or apologize for my position in the Bureau."

"No, you don't. What you do have to do, Harvey, is have an appreciation for what those in that position have to do."

Harvey shrugged and started up from the chair, smoothing out his shirt and tie and saying, "I do have an appreciation for the position you're in. It's getting too dangerous. I'm getting uncomfortable with the whole operation. That's my call."

She could tell he liked that last part.

The stockbroker stopped at the door and said, "I don't see something more concrete soon, we're going to have to pull the plug, reassign you."

My Own Worst Enemy

★ ★ ★ ★ ★

Murray made the left turn off of Northwest Sixty-second Street and stopped short, pulling up near the curb far enough to where he wouldn't be rear-ended if somebody else made the turn. He started to get out, moving on the handle when a red Honda moved past him. He watched it nose into a spot on the curb about four or five cars up, right across the street from 1080. Murray could tell it was a woman at the wheel, seeing the shadow of her hair flip when she looked back to make sure she was in straight.

He didn't move, content to wait for the woman to get her purse and assorted other things she traveled with and get inside before he got out. He wondered if the folks on their porches were paying any attention to him, a white guy in these parts. They had a white neighbor, Rudy Maxa, so maybe they weren't all that surprised by it. Murray could see an older, portly woman—kindly old soul, he thought—staring at him like he'd just landed from another planet. Okay, maybe they weren't used to it. She comes over here, or sends her son, or somebody else comes up to his window wondering what he's doing here, what he'd do was tell them he took the wrong exit off 95. Got all turned around. Make up a story. A story like he was coming to see an old friend that he heard lives on this block.

Murray looked out the windshield and watched a figure in sunglasses and black clothes walking across the street. Funny, she was going right up to the porch to the front of Rudy Maxa's house. Nice legs in that slim skirt; a nice suit jacket that looked like it was cut just for her; black and white two-tone heels, a nice touch. The black hair with auburn highlights.

It kind of made him think of Miranda Mendoza.

Miranda knocked on the screen door and waited, shifting her purse over her shoulder, still looking at the door, waiting for whatever appeared in the opening, her hand on the pistol in the holster cinched in the waistband of her skirt.

She looked away for a moment, the gleam from the windshield of a black car at the end of the block catching her eye. She watched it back up, enough to clear the car in front of it, then whip a u-turn back to the intersection with Northwest Sixty-second Street.

The inside door opened.

Miranda stared through the haze of the screen door, looking at a woman still in her bathrobe and hair curlers.

Well, she's definitely not prettier than me, she thought.

Miranda said, "I'm sorry to disturb you, ma'am, but you are . . . ," thinking about taking her I.D. out.

The woman in her bathrobe took a minute, pulling her robe up around her neck, giving a look like, *Who am I? Who the fuck are you?* The eyes were squinted, the first time they'd seen the sun burning hot today. The nose and forehead crinkled when she said, "Faye Grasso."

No inflection in the voice, sounding unimpressed. Tired.

"You a lawyer?" Faye said, still talking through the screen door.

Miranda shook her head. "No."

Faye looked Miranda up and down, leaning in close to the screen door to get a full look over the wood part that ran perpendicular across the middle, telling Miranda she liked her shoes.

"You too pretty to be with probation," Faye said. "You a cop?"

Miranda smiled. "Sort of."

"What's he done?"

"May I come in?"

Miranda waited while Faye looked at her, then past her—or through her, she couldn't tell—then watched Faye unhook the chain and turn away from the door, waving for Miranda to follow.

Miranda stepped inside and closed the screen and inside door after her. She said thank you when Faye offered her a seat and introduced herself, passing her card to Faye as she looked around the living room: White floral prints on the furniture a light gray from the film built up over time, pizza box and plastic cups on the coffee table, one cup with cigarette butts almost up to the rim.

Faye said, "What kind of trouble Rudy in now?"

"Actually, I'm here about someone else. Maybe a friend, or somebody he does business with, we're not sure of the connection yet. I was wondering if maybe you know him."

Faye waited.

"Jack Murray?"

Faye lit up a cigarette and took a long drag, flicking her ash in that plastic cup. She said, "Jack?" and blew out a stream of smoke. "It's been a long time since I seen him."

"So, you do know him?"

"Sure." Faye drew on her cigarette, nodding, then let the smoke drift from her mouth and waved it away from Miranda's direction. "Him and Rudy go way back." She stopped. "I tell you some shit, what little I know, you ain't looking to use none of that against Rudy, huh?"

Miranda shook her head. "I just want some background information. Part of an ongoing investigation. Rudy won't come up."

"That's all well and good, but Jack Murray shouldn't be coming up, either. Like I say, him and Rudy been working together a long time. All the characters Rudy done brought into our houses, Jack's the only one I ever liked. Wherever we lived, he's the only one with manners. Wipes his shoes off before he come in, don't eat all my food, stuff like that." Faye brought her arms up to her chest, crossing them tight against her chest. "You could do a lot better investigating somebody else. Jack Murray's got class."

Miranda smiled and nodded her head. Okay, so now that she knew that Jack Murray had class, she wondered where to go with it. She could see Faye looking at her, looking bored. There was a commercial that said *Divorce Court* was starting in a few minutes, and she could tell Faye was anxious to see it.

She had to think of something.

"Have you seen Rudy lately?"

Faye shifted in her recliner, pissed off now, back to holding the bathrobe tight up around her neck. "No," she said. "You find that prick, you tell him I need some grocery money."

Miranda watched her, the desperation of wondering what question to ask next giving way to interest. She said, "When's the last time you saw him?"

Faye looked up like the answer was written on the ceiling. "Couple weeks."

"If you don't mind my asking, what was it that you two talked about?" She thought it was the right question, seeing as how it was apparent they didn't see each other all that often.

"Wasn't about my grocery money, I can tell you that."

Miranda waited.

"Aw, he gave me some nonsense about he got this big thing going down, talking like he going to get rich, take me out of this dump."

"He mention Jack in this?"

Faye shrugged. "I don't recall Jack's name coming up."

"How about anybody else?"

Faye's head was cocked at an angle, and her index finger came up from a hand holding her bathrobe at her neck. "Now, I don't want Rudy mixed up in whatever you asking all these questions about."

Miranda told her again that it wouldn't.

"Just this one guy he been hanging around with, guy named Tiras Williams. He's not like Jack at all. Coming up in here with all his thugs, dirtyin' up my house, eating all my food."

Miranda said it to herself, making sure she'd remember it. She said, "How do you spell that?"

"T-i-r-a-s. Only way I know is because I asked Rudy."

Faye put her cigarette out in the plastic cup and lit another one.

"Now that's somebody you should be looking for."

Murray sat parked at an empty parking strip across Northwest Sixty-second at an angle where he could see Faye Grasso's house. The worst part was the waiting. Waiting to see if it actually was her or just his imagination seeing her again. He checked his watch. Five minutes had passed since the last time he checked it. She had been in there for almost thirty minutes. Might as well have been three hours.

Murray thought about going, thought about leaving it, that it had to be somebody else. He told himself it was a coincidence. No big deal, could've been a bill collector. Just back out and be on your way, come back and try again later. He'd have a laugh about it with Faye. But, he didn't. What he did was stare in his rearview mirror as the figure in black came out and stood there, hip cocked, ear on a cell phone. About time.

Then, Murray watched a black Corsica make the right turn onto Faye's street, adjusting his mirror to see the Corsica come to a stop, double-parking roughly where the red Honda was. He could make out a guy in a dark suit, a tall guy, thin with a buzz cut, getting out and leaning against the driver's side door. Not even discreet about it.

He had never seen a bill collector do it like that before.

★ ★ ★ ★ ★

Miranda was holding the screen door in one hand, her cell phone in the other, listening to Natalie Solis tell her what they had on file for Tiras Williams. She said thank you and hung up, Faye's blank stare looking back at her.

"The next time you talk to Rudy," she said, "you tell him to put as much distance between him and Tiras Williams as possible."

Faye took a drag on her cigarette, still holding her robe tight against her body, shaking her head to show Miranda she understood. She said, "I been telling him that forever."

"Well, it's different now. He's in over his head, and I have a feeling it won't end well."

"Anything to do with him usually don't."

Miranda motioned to the black Corsica, wondering why that guy, a young guy she didn't know, was out of his car, overdoing it. He would have to get back in so she could move and he could take her spot.

"I'm going to keep a couple of guys here," she said, wondering alternately if she was going too far and how she would explain this to Harvey if he caught wind of it. She saw Faye squinting past her to the tall, young guy with the buzz cut and aviator sunglasses and said, "In case Rudy comes back with Tiras."

Faye slipped the card Miranda gave her into the pocket of her robe.

"Long as they let him give me my grocery money."

Chapter Nine

Miranda pulled up in front of the house on Northwest Twenty-fourth Avenue, Tiras Williams's house, or at least the last known address she got from the public defender's office, wondering if she even had the right house, if the information was current. They all looked the same, one after another just like on Faye Grasso's block.

She knew she had the right house when she saw a white guy standing outside smoking a cigarette. One, there weren't many white guys in this neighborhood, besides the ones looking to get smack and get out, fast; two, he matched the description Faye gave him; three, he looked like a Rudy. Scrawny, fidgety little fella—about five-seven, as tall as Miranda without shoes—from the look she got before his back showed to her. She watched him walk to the side of the house, lean back against it, bringing one leg up, resting his foot against the siding that was showing its age, nursing his cigarette. Trying hard to look cool or natural, working at it, eyes squinting as he looked around. He half-turned now, thumbs hooked in his pocket, trying out a James Dean impersonation. He angled forward some to look out at the street, a hand running through his hair.

Miranda leaned toward the passenger side window to get a better look, hitting the automatic window button for that side. She saw him look over once, not giving it much. Not expecting to have some good looking chick checking him out. Then, she saw him give her a 'Who me?' look when she waved him over, bringing his hand up to his chest, eyes bulging.

Surprised.

Miranda said, "Rudy?" watching him lean into the window frame.

She watched him hesitate, thinking about it, wondering how she could know him or trying to figure out how he could place her.

Rudy took his hands off the door, running one through his hair before he said, "I think I would've remembered you."

"I dance at Caesar Pelli's club," she said, raising her hand to stroke the bangs away from her face.

Rudy said, "Yeah, I been out there a couple times. Place on Collins, right?"

Miranda smiled and nodded.

Rudy stopped, smiling but not saying a word. His face showed Miranda he was trying to formulate a question.

"How'd you know my name?"

"I heard your name," she said. "You were in there a couple nights ago; one of the girls knew you. I don't remember which one. She was talking about you."

Make him feel important.

"Is that right?"

"Yeah," she said, smiling at him. "I was headed to a friend's house up the street and I saw you. I stopped to look."

Make him feel good.

"A friend? In this neighborhood?" Rudy said, trying to make conversation. "What kind of stuff you looking for?"

She laughed, watching him laugh at his funny line then watched his face look like he had another question.

"So, you're a dancer over there, huh?"

A question like, *Maybe you want to give me a private dance? Just for me?*

Rudy said, "So . . ."

She waited.

Finally, she said, "You know a guy over there, name's Jack Murray?"

Murray watched Rudy lean on the car; watched him slouch his shoulders, run his hands through his hair. And, watching her, Jesus, flipping her hair. What the hell was she doing? Enjoying this?

He stayed about a block-and-a-half behind after turning right off of 12th, not sure if she could see him or if she had on the way over. Pretty sure he was in the clear with Miranda. Pretty sure he was in the clear with Rudy, too; sure that he wouldn't know what he was looking at if he picked his head up and looked down the street.

Man, she sure was chatty. The way she played with her hair, cocked her head when she spoke or smiled when she talked to you. He could see her outline from here, doing all those things. What really got him wondering—or worried, if he was in another mood at another time—was why she was acting that way with Rudy.

The same way she acted with him.

Murray tried not to think about that, still watching Rudy and Miranda, Rudy talking now, Miranda playing with her hair again, listening. He moved down in his seat when Rudy looked back his way before moving back to Miranda. He stayed there, ducking his head now when he noticed Miranda look back. To see what Rudy looked at, he figured. Neither of them gave it much, both turning back quick, still talking.

Murray tried to figure out how they might know each other, going at it for a while now. Maybe they were old friends, just happened to bump into each other—the only white faces in this neighborhood. But, as far as he knew, Rudy didn't have any friends. So that was out.

Okay, they weren't catching up on old times.

Then, what were they talking about?

Rudy said, "Yeah, we work together sometimes, or, I should say, used to work together."

"*Used* to?"

"Yeah," Rudy said, leaning back, trying to get his chest out, get her to notice. "I got tired of carrying his load. We got busted awhile back, on a job."

"Really?" Miranda said, moving up in her seat.

"Cops started chasing us," he said, using his hands to show her what it looked like, one hand in front of the other, palms turned down. "I got to the car first, waited for Jack." Rudy let the chasing hands fall to his side. "But he got scared, laid down, waited to get caught."

"He didn't roll over on you?" She didn't waste any time with it. "While he was in prison, I mean."

"Nah," Rudy said, waving it off, like it was a ridiculous suggestion. "He's not that smart."

"Well, I'm a friend of Jack's. He doesn't seem dumb to me."

Rudy's head jerked back, the light in his head going on, like some kind of recognition. He pushed himself away from the car, trying to get straight up, away from her.

Miranda thought this might have been coming, her reflexes tight, body tense as she grabbed the stomach of Rudy's t-shirt and pulled hard, jamming him into the doorframe. His hair flapped forward, the bangs resting on her forearm as she used her free hand to get her badge.

"What the fuck?" he said, tilting his head up.

"I've seen you around with Tiras Williams lately."

Rudy said, "Then what the fuck you want?" The words trailed off as he got around to noticing the badge resting on the center console.

"I want to know what the hell is going on."

"With what?" Talking to her but staring at the badge.

Miranda held Rudy's shirt, pulling it tighter, her nails helping her claw it. With her free hand, she turned the ignition, giving a tug when she felt Rudy fight and shifted into drive, letting her Honda idle down the curb a few feet. She glanced back and forth between the road and Rudy, hanging on to the window, eyes big like softballs, stumbling to keep up.

She stopped and shifted the car back into park.

"Rudy," Miranda said, trying to get his attention.

"Jesus," he said, straightening out, getting his feet under him. "What?" Raising his hands.

"I'm with the FBI."

She couldn't tell if he was still gathering himself or not sure if what she said had sunk in.

She said his name again, then, "Did you hear what I said?"

He said, "Yeah," nodding, not sure of what else he was supposed to say.

"Look," Miranda said, hoping the tone would calm him down, "I'm not interested in you." Stop him from doing anything stupid. "It's the guy you're with, Tiras Williams."

"What do you want with him?"

"I want to know what he's into."

"Why the fuck should I tell you anything?"

"Well, I could have a SWAT team here in five minutes."

"For what?"

"For starters, this job, whatever it is, that you and Jack were involved in . . ."

"That's not federal."

"I have friends." She watched Rudy's head sink, the hair hanging, then started again. "Second, for conspiring to do whatever it is you're mixed up with this guy to do."

The poor guy, desperate; in a real bind, too, looking back to the house right off Northwest Twenty-fourth. Miranda glanced that way, too. All she could see from here, turned around, looking through the back window, were a couple of windows with faces in them, watching this white boy get dragged down the street by some bitch in a red Honda. She had to look twice to make sure there was no one in a window at Tiras's house. They all looked the same.

"It's up to you," she said.

"Jesus," Rudy said, shaking his head.

She waited.

"It's all Tiras, man," he said. "I got nothing to do with it. I'm telling you."

"Nothing to do with what?"

"The job Jack and I did. We came away with almost twenty-four grand. I took off for the Bahamas after that, got the hell out. Had a run at one of the casinos over there, ran up to a half million."

"Now Tiras has it."

"Yeah," Rudy said. "He wants to use it to buy some guns."

"From who?"

Rudy shrugged.

"Keep going."

"He wants to turn them around, sell to a contact of mine from Atlanta."

"What's your contact's name?"

"Lloyd Bone."

"Rudy," Miranda said, "is Jack involved in any of this?"

Getting to what she really wanted.

He hesitated. "No, not that I know of."

Miranda sat back in the driver's seat, still holding Rudy's shirt, contemplating. Jack wasn't involved. As far as Rudy was aware of. And, she was pretty sure he'd be aware if Jack was involved. Especially if the money they got from a job is what was moving all this.

She said, "Where can I find Jack?"

Rudy hesitated again.

Miranda gave him a tug, saying "Where?" as she did it.

"He stays at the Casita. On Collins, near Fourteenth."

The way it happened, Rudy started talking when Miranda let his shirt go. He started talking about that night with Jack in Coral Gables; talking about him being in that crack house when Tiras came in; even talking about Tommy Smalls.

After he finished, Rudy looked back at Tiras's house. "Look, these guys are fucking animals. They come out here, they're going to know something's up."

Miranda checked the rearview mirror, biting her lip a bit as she watched the front door to Tiras's house open.

"Too late," she said.

Rudy looked back to see the door open. Then, hearing the engine start, turning back just in time to see the red Honda moving away from the curb.

What Rudy did after watching . . . wait, he didn't even get her name. Well, after watching *her* drive away, what he did was look back to Tiras's house, two doors down from where he was now. Tiras was out on the porch, standing still in his t-shirt and green University of Miami mesh shorts, empty hands raised. He could see Lil' Man and Kwame through the screen of the living room window, staring with dumb faces. The kind of look Rudy was getting used to from them. All of them looking at him, Tiras saying something as the other two moved away from the window and came over to Rudy, by himself.

"What the fuck was that?" Tiras said, empty hands raised again.

Rudy didn't say anything, just turned, looking back down the road, wishing he was next to that chick in the car. Going down the road, getting out of there. Man, he wanted to get out of there. *Now.* He was relieved Tiras didn't push it, letting it go at him saying nothing. Until . . .

"C'mon, get your shit."

It was always something.

"Why?" Rudy said, his voice soft, knowing he wasn't looking forward to what was coming next.

"We going shopping."

Jack Murray came up in his seat to watch Tiras and Rudy standing in front of somebody else's yard, talking. Before that, even. When Miranda pulled away. Now he saw Tiras, the back showing to Jack, doing the talking. Arms moving up and down. Hand gestures. Rudy not doing much of anything, getting bitched out.

They must've been into it pretty good because Murray was sure he went unnoticed as his Taurus moved past them.

They didn't even look up.

Chapter Ten

There was Rudy, the white boy, and Tiras and Lil' Man and Kwame in the living room, getting ready. Kwame punched Lil' Man in the chest a few times, getting him primed, Rudy thought, until Lil' Man told him to stop, that it was starting to hurt, seriously. Rudy's gaze moved over to the guns and boxes of bullets on the coffee table, watching Tiras slide a magazine into a pistol that he didn't know the make of.

Funny way to go shopping.

"I see you looking," Tiras said, sliding a magazine in another pistol, not looking up when he said it. "Eyes bugging out, wondering what the hell you about to get into."

Rudy nodded, saying, "I don't care," trying to sound nonchalant about it, show Tiras that he didn't really give a damn. Not give him the satisfaction that he maybe just shit his pants.

It's just that he was starting to wonder exactly what "shopping" meant.

Tiras said, "You don't care? So, you Mister Cool now, huh?" Laughing at him. "Nah, you ain't got to worry about no gunplay, anything like that."

Rudy's eyebrow arched, forehead crinkling, nodding his head like he was interested, like he knew that was coming.

"We going see Malik, a nigga that lives around the way. Came up together in the John Does. Shit, we go back farther than that. Pop Warner football." Tiras racked the slide on another gun, then set it on the coffee table. "You believe that?" Tiras said, looking off like he was remembering some time long ago.

Rudy shrugged, not sure what Tiras thought he would say.

Tiras picked up the pistol off the coffee table, turned it end over end and handed it to Rudy, butt-first.

"Don't worry," Tiras said. "He's an old friend."

Lil' Man backed Tiras's Escalade into a narrow alley off Northwest Fifteenth Aveune, stopping on the street and putting his hazards on, waving the traffic around him before doing it. Tiras freaked when he thought Lil' Man came too close to the brick wall and Rudy thought, Jesus, he was going to maybe shoot him in the nuts right there. It could've happened, Tiras hitting some meth before they left the house. Kwame, too.

They were between two stores, one with a sign that said it was Bar B's Grocery and Take-Out with bars on the windows. The other one was a men's store that sold what Rudy thought looked like zoot suits and flashy costume jewelry. No sign in the window, but it had bars, too.

As soon as they squeezed out of the truck—Tiras making sure to tell everybody to watch how they opened the door, that he was gonna have whoever's ass scratched his paint job on the brick wall—they started up a small staircase going into the back of the zoot suit store. Tiras gave a knock, some kind of secret code.

The biggest human being—this guy was black, but whatever color—Rudy had ever seen appeared in the doorway, listening to Tiras tell him why they were here.

Rudy followed Tiras in expecting to see an office with a desk and a filing cabinet, cardboard boxes, a computer that was new in nineteen-eighty-six. Maybe even one of those zoot suits hanging in a clear plastic bag in the corner. The latest model.

What he got looked like a nightclub crossed with a living

room. Streaky neon lighting bouncing off a disco ball. Two plush couches, three-seaters each. There was a chick with legs up to there and a skirt short enough to see them on the couch nearest the door, looking left as they went inside. Wait, there was a second woman coming out of a bathroom, the sound of a toilet flushing behind her. Gold diggers is what Rudy saw them as, girls who loved being around guys like this for what they could get out of it.

The giant that answered the door was standing in front of it now, closing it behind him as Kwame stepped in. Two others almost as big as him were around, milling about.

It surprised Rudy that the guy Tiras moved to was the smallest guy in the room. He said, "Malik," and held his hand out. Malik took it and pulled Tiras close to him, hugging Tiras while his eyes looked out at Kwame, then the rest of him moving to Kwame after sliding away from Tiras. Giving Kwame some sort of secret handshake like they played Pop Warner football together, too.

Tiras said to Mailk, "That's Lil' Man," watching Malik giving Lil' Man a curious look.

Malik said, "I know you, man?"

"Marion Williams," Tiras said, cutting Lil' Man off. "He used to play right guard at Miami. Blew out his knee senior year against Florida State."

"MCL, PCL, ACL," Lil' Man said. "All my ligaments."

"Might be it," Malik said, nodding his head like he wasn't sure if that was it or not.

"Spent a couple years on the Dolphins' practice squad," Tiras said, looking back at Lil' Man, standing still, looking mean while Tiras gave his resume. "Mean motherfucker."

Malik nodded, approving, then moved over to Rudy, giving him the up-and-down once-over.

Tiras said, "This here's Rudy Maxa."

Malik didn't say anything, didn't even bother with it, just gave Tiras a look like, *What the fuck is this?*

Rudy could tell by Tiras's face that he was embarrassed. Fuck him, man. *You're not embarrassed with my money,* Rudy told himself. *Shit. Wasn't for my money, you wouldn't be here.* He felt like saying it out loud, putting his two cents in, being the odd man out, watching these four dudes whooping it up. Speaking some fucking language he didn't even understand.

Rudy started walking towards them, feeling himself being looked at, when he heard Malik say, "I suppose y'all carrying?" and he stopped.

Malik pointed to the floor, wanting Tiras to take off the pistol taped to his ankle. He did it, neither of them saying anything about it, it was just business, and set it on a countertop next to three others that Lil' Man and Kwame had already set up there.

"You, too?" Malik said, turning to Rudy, waiting for him to say or do something.

Rudy didn't say anything, just took the pistol he had tucked in his front pocket and set it on the countertop.

It didn't take long after the guns were on the table that Malik opened for business. He walked over to a blank portion of the office wall, Kwame and Lil' Man wondering what he was doing, Tiras's eyes showing that he knew exactly what was happening.

The blank portion of the wall opened and Malik went in, flipping a light switch as he did it, motioning for everybody to follow. Lil' Man and Kwame ooh-ed and ah-ed looking at the wall mounted display cases—or at least their version of it considering they had to act like they'd seen all this before. Tiras was silent, his gaze moving across the display cases, eyes squinting like he was deciding what he wanted first. Stopping on a pair of Heckler & Koch nine-millimeter MP5s, Tiras said, "Damn, nigga. What the fuck you need all this for?"

Malik said, "For silly brothers like you," smiling now, winking, "coming in here, needing this or that." Malik looked around the walls, wiping a smudge from a piece of display glass in front of a 12-gauge shotgun. "Yeah, I get ten, twenty niggas a day in here, needing some kind of shit."

Tiras lifted a Colt .45 semiautomatic off the wall through a piece of the glass wall that was already slid open. Looking down the sight, he said, "This shit sure 'nuff stop some motherfucker mouthing off."

Malik nodded, watching Tiras pass the .45 off to Lil' Man, then Lil' Man pass it off to Kwame so they could look down the sight and pretend-fire, just like Tiras did.

While Kwame held up the .45 again and aimed it, Malik opened a closet and pulled out what looked like a steamer trunk, rolling it out on wheeled brackets.

"You still after those TECs?"

Tiras looked up, nodding.

"You know, you could do a lot better with some AKs," Malik said, opening the trunk, "or some forty-five caliber M3 submachine guns. There's some made by General Motors. They actually say it's a very pleasant gun to shoot, like they proud of that." Now Malik had picked up a pistol off the wall mount, held it up and aimed, closing one eye, tilting his head and looking down the sight. "Maybe some Glocks." He replaced it on the wall. "It's a good little piece."

"I know all about that shit, brother," Tiras said. "And, you right. But, I got this dude coming down from Atlanta say he wants the TEC."

Malik went on about how cheap the TEC was, good to turn a buck but that was about it. "Good for sprayin' and prayin', though. You can turn it, shoot it sideways. Got that high pitch with the thirty-two round mag, do more scaring a nigga than actually hurting him. And, they look good with the cooling holes." He let it go, getting tired about arguing about which automatic weapon could kill somebody deader.

"Got my money?" he said.

Tiras told Lil' Man, "Go on out to the car and get the man his money."

Lil' Man wasn't out the door before Tiras put his hand on Rudy's chest and backed him out of the closet, closing the door as he saw Rudy reach one of the sofas.

"I got something else I need done," Tiras said, his eyes moving across the gun cabinet before holding on Malik.

"I'm always looking for work."

"Well," Tiras said, grinning now, "how about I throw in some change, and you take out some of my garbage."

"What kinda garbage we talking about?"

"White kind," Tiras said. "Motherfucker's riding my ass." He motioned toward the wall separating the gun office from the regular office. "Old associate of my boy out there."

"And, he you property now."

"*Exactly*," Tiras said, pumping his fist and forefinger, glad that he could find someone that could empathize with him. "And, what makes this situation vol-a-til is that my next deal," carrying his hand over in a semi-circle, "depends on his being with me, not with this other dude."

"What's this white boy's name?"

"Jack Murray. He stay at the Casita. On Collins, near Fourteenth."

Malik stopped before saying anything. He tilted his head and said, "How much we talking?"

"Extra five thousand."

Malik stuck out his bottom lip and nodded.

"You got that five on you?"

Murray sat on the wicker sofa in his apartment, staring at the mostly bare white walls, sometimes focusing on the prints of flowers hanging up over the bed, full of vibrant colors. That's what the lady told him when he first moved in—that they were vibrant colors. They looked orange to him.

He raised his voice to Nicky Silva, in the kitchen rifling through the refrigerator, that he could have a beer if they had any left.

"I prefer Grey Goose, maybe a nice blended scotch," Murray heard Nicky say, "but it's a little early for me," looking at his gold pocket watch, trying to sound like fucking James Bond. Only with a New Jersey accent that he was trying hard to lose but that still popped up from time to time.

Murray took a swig from an open Natural Light and his face puckered up. "Man, I haven't had this shit since I was in high school."

Nicky was still talking about all the brand name liquor he liked, or preferred, and that he didn't like the bloating he got from beer when Murray walked back into the living area. Then, Murray stared at him while Nicky wiped his forehead and worked at keeping his silk shirt and slacks unwrinkled. Primping his hair in a pocket mirror. Worried about that at a time like this.

Nicky said, "You ever have a girl up here?"

Murray shrugged, bringing his Natural Light down, ready to speak, when . . .

"Only reason I ask is because when I was coming up here, an old lady asked me if I was with Hospice. Man, I don't know if they all heard her, although I don't know how unless they had those hearing aids turned way up *and* had their ear to the door, but there must've been about three or four doors open, looking at me, waiting for an answer. I tell her 'no, ma'am,' because she's a cute old lady and I'm a nice guy. I walk a little more, another thinks I'm her grandson bringing her oxygen. They're everywhere, man. Watching everything. That's all they have to do. Wonder what you're doing. Can you imagine what kind of ruckus you'd cause bringing some woman past them? It's like a gauntlet."

Murray shook his head, not wanting to get into it even if he did bring somebody to his room. He sat there, waiting for Nicky to talk . . .

"Lucky for me, I don't have that problem. Man, I bring a different one home every night, give 'em the old Silva Bullet," grabbing his crotch (which Murray thought was weird, doing that in front of another man), "they would bust those hearing aids right out with all the screaming goes on at my place." Laughing at the funny name for his schlong. Smiling as he waited for a reaction from Murray.

Murray didn't laugh but did give him a smirk. Not because he thought it was funny but because he wondered if Gina was one of those screamers, positive from what he saw earlier that they were fucking. What would be funny would be seeing how he explained it to Caesar if it ever came out. Hilarious.

"Only problem I ever had was after those three black assholes came through here, loud as all get out, in the middle of the night."

Nicky shook his head. "Manager ask you about that?"

Murray's cheeks bulged out, filled with beer, as he shook his head. He swallowed and said, "No. But, the only reason I'm still here's because Caesar stepped in."

Nicky sat up, looking at Murray, and said, "What are we looking at?"

Murray knew what he meant. "Three guys in a house off Northwest Twenty-fourth, over in Liberty City."

"Liberty City? Shit. You went over there?"

"I wouldn't know where to find him if I hadn't."

Nicky said, "I hear they eat people over there, especially a white guy like you. They'll skewer you right up. Put an apple in your mouth and turn you round and round over a fire."

"You're not scared, are you?" Murray said, watching Nicky grin and shake his head, squinting his eyes in a look that told Murray, *Hell no, I'm not scared*. Murray said, "Guy like you, you've probably done this a lot."

Nicky blew out of his mouth, nodding, then tugged at his trousers, trying to protect the crease down the front.

Murray said, "Anybody I heard of?"

It was starting to get under his skin a little bit, Nicky Silva feeling like he was being tested by this Jack Murray that he hadn't heard that much about.

Murray heard Nicky rattle off a couple of names. Guys he didn't know or wouldn't know, but that wasn't the point.

"How about you?" Nicky said, sitting up, grinning. Giving Murray some attitude in his voice.

"Never had to use a gun in my life."

Nicky waited for Murray to say something else, like he was expecting a story behind that, then said, "Guys are gonna be hopped up on something anyway," checking his watch, "this time of day, won't even see it coming."

Murray stared at the guy's perfect hair, remembering Caesar telling him that Nicky was all he could spare: "My boys need rest. I got something going on tonight, and I don't want them grabassin', bragging about some jig they did this afternoon." Pause. "I'm spread thin."

Sitting back, nursing his beer, Murray was seeing Miranda in different ways. Just like that night when Tiras showed up. Except now he wasn't imagining what it would be like to wake up with her. He was remembering her in different, other, ways: catching her changing in the dressing room, seeing her up close that first time with her smiling back at him; noticing her legs when they were at Fairchild Gardens, and watching them move in her skirt as she walked back to her car, looking for her pantyline under there. He was hearing her, too. Hearing her voice tell him her real name. Miranda. He really liked the sound of it. Or, the inflection in her tone when she gave him her number. Like he was nineteen again. He could tell by the way she talked to him that he wasn't just a customer to her, the way some dancers get closer to big tippers. Make them think there was something more there. Guys like Rudy went for that. How else could they be so buddy-buddy? Of course, they didn't look too friendly when she was dragging him down the street.

It kept nagging at him, though. Rudy just didn't have any friends, especially ones as good looking as she was. And, not enough money to be a big tipper. So, if that was the case—why was she there?

"I'm ready," Nicky said. "I want to get this out of the way."

Murray didn't really feel like getting up. It was getting late in the day, twilight on its way, a ray of late afternoon light coming through the window just below where the shade had been pulled down. He was feeling relaxed, ready for another beer, wanting to get a buzz. Not worry about this shit.

Right as he thought about that last part, Murray heard two sounds: a knock on the door and Nicky pulling back the hammer on his pistol.

Then, Nicky's head, with that big, coifed hair-do, appeared around the partition separating the front area from the living area.

"You expecting somebody?"

"I need to talk to you."

Murray didn't like the sound of that.

He stood there, looking at Miranda in the doorframe still in that nice black skirt, holding the door open. He let her in at the same time that she asked to come in and turned to look for

Nicky Silva.

When Nicky came out from the bedroom—Murray saw that he had tucked his gun away—Murray motioned to him, saying, "Miranda, this is Nick."

Not Nicky.

She said, "Can we talk in private?"

It was getting worse.

Murray said, "Nick's going to wait outside," and saw Nicky Silva give him a look.

Murray followed Miranda into the living area, watching her look over the walls, the furniture, glance back into the kitchen at the dirty plates in the sink. He felt like telling her, *Hey, I was gonna do the dishes but I got rousted out of the house at two o'clock in the morning and haven't been able to get around to it yet.* She sat on the sofa, trying to find a position on the wicker that was comfortable. Still looking around, making judgments.

Murray sat down. Not too close to her so he could notice her legs without it being obvious. Man, that body. He felt the tension and wanted to say something to cut out the awkwardness. Not something forward, like that he wanted to hump her. Nothing like that. Just something to keep it light.

He could see Miranda getting in position, straightening out, readying herself for whatever she had to say. All that time she was taking, Murray still couldn't get anything out, scared to death.

"Jack, it's about Rudy Maxa."

Murray hunched his shoulders, feeling like he was breathing again for the first time in a couple of minutes. He took a second trying to figure out what to say then just put on a blank stare.

Miranda waited for him to say something. When he didn't, she said, "I followed you to Faye Russo's last night."

"Why?"

Like he had something to hide.

She took a minute and now he felt like it was his turn to say something. He didn't see the logic because he just did say something, and it got him in the hole as far as he was concerned.

Miranda said, "Where's your bathroom?"

Murray pointed in the general direction of the bedroom and was about to tell her that it was the only one before he felt her brush past him. He heard the door close and wondered how long she would be in there. He was still floored with the Faye Russo thing, having time to put two and two together. She must've followed him from Fairchild. Sneaky. Which means she was probably thinking about doing it while they were sitting there talking about Steve McQueen movies. Mistrust; misunderstanding; miscommunication. They had only met a few days ago, but, man, this was starting to feel like an honest-to-God relationship.

And, if that was the case, Murray knew there was more to come. She wasn't in there recovering. She was in there reloading. He thought maybe he could talk her down, maybe get her back. He was a good listener—it was always best to just be quiet with a woman. Open your mouth, you get yourself in trouble. He'd done that already, and she ran into the bathroom.

But when he saw her come back and lean into the bedroom doorframe, not saying anything, he wasn't sure of anything.

She sat back on the sofa and said, "Jack, I'm with the FBI."

"Why are you telling me this?"

"Because I trust you, Jack. I trust you enough to tell you that I'm an FBI agent assigned to Caesar's club so I can find out about his organization. That's what I've been doing there."

Murray hesitated. "Miranda . . ."

She cut him off, which was okay by him because he wasn't sure what he was going to say next.

"Look, Jack, I'm not stupid."

Murray wanted to say that he knew she wasn't stupid, give

her a compliment at a time like this.

She said, "I know you and Rudy have a history. You feel like he owes you. You're looking for some sort of retribution . . . whatever. But, he's in too deep now, running with a crowd he's not accustomed to. I just want to be sure you're not part of it."

Murray hesitated, then leaned in to touch her hand.

"I'm not," he said.

"Then you're not after Tiras Williams."

Murray shrugged, letting it go. He was just delaying the inevitable; sooner or later she'd ask it again. Then, she'd ask even more questions. Finally, he said, "Are you?"

Miranda nodded and said, "Yeah. And, when I catch up to him, everybody around him is going to fall," wiping the corner of her right eye, dry now, but Murray could see a little welling in there. "I don't want you to fall, Jack."

"I won't."

"So, you are after him?"

There it was.

"Miranda . . ."

"What is it, Jack?" she said. "Some old vendetta? Two guys out in the yard with something to prove? You think if you lay your hands on what he's got that you'll feel vindicated? That you've won?"

Well, half the money was his.

A third time, he said, "Miranda . . ."

"Well, I'll tell you, Jack. You won't. You'll end up back in jail or dead."

Murray watched her get up, wondering if she had gotten out everything she wanted to. Miranda stopped before reaching the door, taking a deep breath and smoothing out her skirt. He could tell it was coming to an end, this round. And, he had taken a flurry of body blows right from the bell. He didn't know what to say to calm her—or if it was better that he just didn't say anything. He felt he did a good job of listening, though. The only thing that kept him in the conversation.

After he waited it out, she said, "You have my number," cocking her hip, "call me later."

It wasn't long after Miranda was gone that Nicky showed up. He came back to the sofa and sat down a couple of spaces away from Murray.

"What was that all about?"

Murray sat there, digesting what just happened. Nicky's words not registering.

"Lady troubles?" Nicky said.

"It's a girl from the club," Murray said, taking a couple of seconds to figure out his cover story. Then, "She's all pissed off, thinking I'm checking out some of the newer girls coming through."

"You got to watch that, Jack." Nicky settled back, preparing to give sage advice. "You have to lay down the law, right off the bat. Take me for instance . . ." Murray tuned out while Nicky Silva told him his rules for handling women, then came back in for the end, in time to hear Nicky say, "She pulls that shit in the club, with a lot of people around, man, it's not going to end pretty."

If it would have been a regular situation, with some emotional young twenty-something girl, that would have made sense. Murray nodded, saying, "I'll take care of it."

Yeah, but how? It was starting to get to him. The whole Miranda business. FBI? Shit. He hadn't even thought about it that far, still focusing on the fact that it was slipping away. Thinking about what he could say to get her back, rewind time a little bit.

There was other work to do, anyway. Something else to think about, take his mind off that worry. Murray grabbed his .22

from under the seat cushion, popped up, and looked at Nicky. "You ready to go?"

Chapter Eleven

"Her name's Faye Grasso," Miranda said. "The house is in her name, on Northwest Sixty-ninth, in the Liberty City area. Rudy Maxa's the boyfriend. I'm not sure how long they've been together but, judging by our conversation, they go back a ways."

They were in Bill Cecil's kitchen, having coffee. Bill having his after just finishing dinner, Mrs. Cecil being really nice about Miranda's intrusion. Even offering some key lime pie before she shuffled off to the TV room.

"Tell me again how you came by this?"

"I followed Jack Murray over there yesterday afternoon. You remember him? He's the manager at the club."

Bill Cecil nodded. Sipping, he said, "So, you've got two guys sitting in front of a house on Northwest Sixty-ninth?" He sat back and folded his arms, watching Miranda nod her head, using his tongue to pick his teeth. "Where'd you get these guys?"

"A couple of new guys sitting around with nothing to do. Nobody's gotten to them yet but they're itching to do something. They even said, 'Yes, ma'am.' " Miranda put her hand to her chest. "They called *me* 'ma'am.' "

"Was this Jack Murray fella running something over for Caesar?"

Miranda shook her head.

"What was he doing over there then?"

See, this is why she wanted to come over. Better to talk to Bill, talk it out face to face. He looked kind of like her dad, so it was easier in person. It would be too hard to fit in on a cell phone while she was driving anyway.

"I wasn't sure at first . . ."

The ride over gave her time to smooth this part out.

"You ever hear the name Tiras Williams?"

"Can't say that I have," Bill Cecil said, sipping his coffee. "Why?"

"That's what I've been getting to. I want off the Caesar Pelli investigation."

"So, the guys sitting in front of that house—Jack Murray, the new guy, Williams . . . none of these guys have anything to do with Caesar?"

Miranda shook her head and started again.

"It's alright," Bill Cecil said, putting a hand up. "I was going to recommend you be taken off anyhow."

"Why?" Miranda said, getting up. She took Bill's cup and poured his full. She took half a cup, served her boss and sat down again. She watched him take a sip, his head lowered over the table, and waited for him to talk.

"Well," Bill Cecil said, taking his time, "I've never been comfortable with your assignment there. You going undercover there? In a titty bar?" He felt himself getting excited and asked Miranda to excuse his language. He settled down, sitting back and crossing his legs, sipping again and said, "It was a damn fool thing to do."

"It was the best way to find out about the operation, right?"

Bill said, "I thought so at the time. Looking back, I was railroaded into that. Once that little bastard got everybody excited, everything ran downhill."

"Where do we go from here?" That's what she said out loud, but, it was funny, the first thing she thought was, *How am I going to see Jack?*

"I have a friend in the Miami Beach P.D., Matthew Reyes.

You remember Matthew, huh?"

Miranda thought about it for a second then said, "Matt Reyes." Searching more. "Yeah, young guy. Looks like he wears makeup, foundation. Takes a long time doing things. You know, like straightening his tie or buffing his shoes."

"Yeah, he's a bit of a dandy."

"What's he got?"

"What he has is a C.I., a guy that got busted on a possession with intent about a year ago. Guy was on probation for a domestic violence call two years before that in Fort Lauderdale. They pleaded down, he went to work for Matt. Name's Ed, maybe Eddie, I can't remember, and he works at your club, too."

"Ed? The bouncer?"

"You know him?"

"Yeah, he's a real nice guy. Some asshole gets handsy, thinking his one dollar bill is going to get him laid, Ed was always there to put that guy on his ass." Miranda took a sip.

Bill Cecil said, "A real sweetheart."

Miranda watched her boss get up from the table and go over to the French doors, staring out at the bay. Then, sip coffee and stare. Watched him sip and stare until she said, "What's going on?"

Bill Cecil hiked up his khakis and said, "He's got a tip that Caesar's going to be in Allapattah tonight. Something's coming in and he wants to be there, personally. Matt has those details."

"That's a ways outside the beach."

Bill Cecil nodded.

Miranda smiled.

"That's where we, or, I should say, you come in. There's bound to be a pissing contest over jurisdiction, if there hasn't been already. If somebody's there that's federal . . ."

"Everybody keeps it in their pants."

"Considering your familiarity with the specifics," he said, leaning against the counter, "you could act as the Bureau's presence."

She liked it, the thought of being the Bureau's "presence." Normally, it would have sounded like a bunch of double-talk—until it was used to describe her. Hey, five weeks ago she was thought of well enough to take nearly all of her clothes off and dance around, listening around corners and looking through peepholes when she could.

Bill Cecil set his cup down in the sink, Miranda hearing the clanking sound of it against the dinner plates already in there as she turned for the door leading out to the garage.

"Reyes'll be expecting your call," Bill said, wondering if she was going to ask him anything else. He held the door open, let Miranda through then went himself and closed it after. "We have to clear up this thing about those guys in front of that house, though."

"What do you want me to do?"

"I want you to get them out of there. That wasn't authorized, and if Turner gets wind of it, he'll tear you a new one. You know how he is."

Miranda could hear it, too: every regulation she had violated; the chain of command she'd disrespected; every dollar in the budget and every man-hour she'd wasted, his favorite . . . He was good at counting the beans.

She said, "I'll take care of it."

Miranda turned for her car, thinking, Faye Russo's house wasn't too far out of the way from here on the way to Matt Reyes's office.

Miranda told the two young guys sitting in front of Faye Russo's house that they needed to get over to Northwest Twenty-fourth Avenue. She told them they needed to look for a black

Escalade out front so they'd know they were watching the right place, that the houses all looked alike and they could spend the next couple of days watching an abandoned house if they weren't sure.

She thought it might not be a bad idea—her unit busting Tiras Williams's crew. Maybe her primary target was Caesar Pelli's organization, but one of south Florida's rising amateur criminals was a hell of an ancillary benefit. Bill Cecil could push the brass if he had to. Just give him a nudge. He could tell them it was an unexpected bonus for her career and the Bureau's p.r. Another successful female agent. If she had to, she could give the credit to Harvey Turner.

And, since Williams wasn't connected with the Pelli group, it probably wouldn't jeopardize her standing there anyhow. Providing Bill Cecil spoke to the right people.

Plus, she could get Tiras off Jack's ass.

Hey, she said she'd take care of it.

Soon as Tiras pulled in his driveway, he told Lil' Man and Kwame he wanted the gun cases out of his truck. First thing. Rudy, too. He could carry the small boxes.

"I ain't rollin' with my retirement in the back of my car," he said, unlocking the shed at the back of the house. He freaked when Lil' Man lost his grip going lengthwise through the door, a corner of the wood box splintering a little when it hit the ground.

Later, there was Tiras, Lil' Man, and Kwame sitting in the living room, getting high. Rudy was sitting away from them, wandering around every so often until Tiras would tell him to sit down. After the third time, Rudy said, "Whaddya want me to do? Sit down all the time?" Frowning.

"Exactly what I want you to do," Tiras said, passing his joint to Kwame. "Sit your ass down and stay there."

Rudy gave him a snicker and said, "What the fuck?" Not sure, or not caring, if Tiras heard it.

"So you don't up and take off on me."

Tiras was feeling relaxed, talkative, asking Kwame what he was going to do with his cut. Kwame talked about limos and bitches and fur coats and bitches. A house with a swimming pool. And bitches. Nevermind that, like Rudy was figuring earlier, his cut would top out at about five grand.

"I'm about to make a shitload off these cheap ass TEC-9s," Tiras said, not waiting to hear what Lil' Man was going to do with his share. "Gonna quadruple my money. *Quadruple*, nigga." Eyes squinting, trying to put a point on it. "This go right, I'm gonna parlay it. Do it again, sell to them boys out in West Palm, Lake Worth. Got some evil motherfuckers out in Lake Worth, you know that. Quadruple my money on all that. Just keep building. Man, can you imagine? Do the math on that."

Rudy wondered, considering what they were going to get, if they actually were doing the math on it.

Tiras was riding that good feeling now, bragging about the organization he was setting up. He used the word "parlay" again, kicking back and taking another hit. Talking now about shipping TECs to Columbia, that he personally knew that's what they used down there; AK-47s to Nigeria. He was going to muscle whoever it was supplying the warlords over there out of business.

Going worldwide.

He turned to Rudy.

"Call your man."

"We're coming up on it," Murray said. "There's his car." Now Murray was smirking, wondering what the hell that pair of headlights was coming up the other side of the street. He could hear Nicky talking, but he was only half-listening, looking around but trying hard to see if it was Miranda at the wheel over those headlights. He frowned when the headlights got close enough that he could tell it was just like that black Corsica in front of Faye Grasso's house.

Yeah, it could be another one.

But what were the odds?

Nicky said, "What do you want me to do?"

Murray told him to pull over, that they were still far enough away where they didn't look so suspicious. He watched the Corsica creep down the street like the driver was looking at house numbers then stop, back up and cut the lights.

After watching the Corsica for a few seconds, waiting for someone to get out, Nicky said, "What do you think that's all about?"

Murray didn't say anything, letting it go but putting a hand on Nicky's arm so he wouldn't open the door and set the dome light on. Keep cool, like they were just sitting and waiting too.

"I think those are cops," Murray said, his voice slow, still trying to figure out if he knew the car.

"You think?" Nicky said, looking at the Corsica then back at Murray. "You think it might be about Tommy Smalls?"

"I'm not sure," Murray said. "I'm not even sure if they're watching Tiras or somebody else. Around here, it could be anybody."

"Well, I'm not going in there, start popping people with the possibility of the police outside."

"You? I wouldn't have guessed it," Murray said, still looking at headlights and parked cars, saying it in a way that Nicky wouldn't get the joke.

"We may as well go." Nicky guided his Nissan Maxima past what Murray was sure now was the same Corsica he had seen in front of Faye Grasso's house earlier. The feds, still wearing their sunglasses. Even at night. Nicky followed Murray's directions to make a block and come out heading for I-95. "I'll take you back to your place. Tomorrow, you can talk to Caesar about it."

"I'll see what he says," Murray said, staring off at the lights across the Julia Tuttle in the distance.

"Those cops might've saved us the trouble for now," Nicky said. "But, he's not going to let it go at that."

Matthew Reyes already had the Sunshine State Lock and Pawn under surveillance by the time Miranda got there. She found him in a Ford Taurus parked on Northwest Fourteenth Avenue, near enough to the corner of Northwest Thirty-fourth Street to give them a clear view of the front door.

Half-past eight in the evening, the closed sign went up. Reyes sent a guy up to the front door to knock on it, make up a story and give some shit about them closing up a half hour before their sign said. That got nothing but a white man's face at the window saying that they were closed. Reyes's man said he could see that. Why weren't they open is what he wanted to know. He kept at it, and the guy came back one more time and told him they were closed and that was it. Closed because they wanted to be closed.

Reyes told his guy not to press it. Just knock a couple of times, see who answers the door, maybe get somebody different a second time.

"Roger that," Reyes said, a voice coming over his ear piece as Reyes watched his man walk away from the door, around the block and disappear. Reyes moved his binoculars back to the front of the store, thinking he saw something move. Yeah, a shape in the window, younger man this time, peeking through the burglar bars and turning out the store light.

"Waiting for the boss," Reyes said. "So he can come pick up his gold-plated diaper."

"It's called a backflap, designed to shield an ancient warrior's backside," Miranda said.

"I know that. I'm just making a joke."

"It's not a joke." She didn't want to come off like a hard-on. But Matt was still a young guy, aggressive, hungry for a juicy collar. A stolen artifact may not have been sexy enough for him. "Stolen artifacts are second only to drugs in terms of contraband trafficked through the U.S. You know that?"

"No, I didn't," he said, making a face.

"You take this backflap plus the three other pieces of gold chest armor you told me about," she said, turning to him. "He could go before a grand jury and get twenty years max for each. Even if he doesn't get the max, he'll get enough to put him away for the rest of his life."

"I guess you're right," Reyes said, shifting in his seat. "That's why it's got to be tonight. It's the first time someone might be able to catch him at the scene, laying his hands on illegal contraband, in," thinking about it, "longer than I've been around."

"My guess is ten years. He doesn't come out much anymore."

"Yeah, but tonight he's getting a gold diaper from Peru."

Nicky dropped Murray off at the corner of Sixteenth, across from the Loews Hotel. This time of night the traffic was picking up on Collins, and Nicky wanted to turn off on Sixteenth and head back to Arthur Godfrey Road. Murray said it was fine, that he actually wanted a walk to clear his head and think about how he was going to break it to Caesar.

Murray moved through the sidewalk crowds on Collins, young people dressed up to go somewhere. He made his way through a crosswalk at Fifteenth, almost getting run over by a Suburban while staring at a girl passing in the other direction. He walked past the front of the Casita on his way to the

Chevron next door for a six-pack. He was feeling like a Heineken, something other than the Natural Light in his fridge.

When he passed the alley adjacent to the Casita he saw a white El Dorado pulled all the way in. Just like Tiras Williams did. Murray took a moment, trying to count the number of heads through the tinted glass. Not much luck with that. The glass was too dark. Murray backed off, out of sight from the alleyway, and sat down on the bench at the front of the building. He felt for the .22 tucked into the stomach pocket of his hooded sweatshirt.

He sat there, trying to figure what to do next. He could wait it out. Maybe whoever it was would get tired of waiting and go home. He could wait right here, and they could back out right past him. They would never know who he was. Dammit, this is where he lived. Why should *he* have to wait because of these assholes?

No, he had a plan. The old element of surprise. First, he could turn on the kitchen light so they could see it. That had to be their signal, the only way to know he was home. Tiras probably told them which window to look for. Then, watch for whoever got out, run down the back stairs and grab whoever was left. Just like he did with Rudy. These guys were going to do things the same way. They weren't smart enough not to. Unless . . .

Somebody was already up there.

Murray walked through the Casita lobby and up the stairs to the second floor. He tried to keep his steps light, his running shoes squeaking against the floor as he heard sounds coming from rooms as he passed them. Old folks watching television or playing cards. A young tourist couple having sex. He came up on his door, walking even softer the closer he got to it. He felt the door handle, jiggling it slow. Not a real surprise that it was locked. Considering somebody could have locked it after going in. He looked at the bottom of the door, trying to find light coming from inside. It was dark. Yeah, if someone was sitting in there, it would be dark.

Murray pulled out the .22, a Targa, from his sweatshirt pocket. Somebody somewhere sometime had told him it was good for up-close work. Not that he ever wanted to be close enough to anybody that he needed a gun that was just right for that . . . if he ever had to shoot somebody. He had been saved the trouble once tonight.

Maybe not a second time, though.

Murray unlocked the door, his shoes squeaking across the tile as he moved through the door to the dining-L. His heart was beating fast, damn, about ready to pop right out of his chest. He listened close, bringing his head up to where the cabinets stopped and the opening led to the living room. He didn't hear anything, but maybe the other guy was hiding, sneaking around real quiet, too. Murray looked over the countertop and didn't see anybody.

He waited.

Got tired of it, tired of the nervousness, and belly-crawled over to the doorframe leading into the bedroom. It was a risk, a guy jumps out of the shadows, he'll catch you in a bad position, on your belly like that. He stopped in the doorframe and extended his arms out in front, the .22 in his right hand. He could see the whole of the small room at once, nobody there. He aimed the pistol at the bathroom door, hoping to catch the guy coming out. If there was anyone in there.

Murray got on his haunches, far enough away from the window now where he couldn't be seen. It was fucking scary, man, creeping around in the dark, in the quiet, trying to find somebody before he could jump out and do something to you.

He got to the bathroom door and didn't move. It gave him

the angle to see the stand-up shower. The door was closed. But, it was always closed unless you were using it. Maybe that was the idea. Wait for him to get home and jump in the shower. Bam. Leave him there, in his bare ass, lying in his own blood.

Well, Murray thought he'd oblige them to a point, taking off his running shoes so the squeak on the tile wouldn't give him away. He took a couple of steps and was right next to the shower door. Godammit, man, this was some scary shit.

Fuck it. Just do it.

Murray swung the door open and crouched down, thinking that whoever was in there would be aiming from the hip and the shot might go over his head. The door hit the wall and swung back before Murray realized the shower was empty.

Shit.

Murray slumped back onto the floor, not knowing if he was going to have a heart attack or piss himself. He stayed there, in the dark, staring at the wall. He wanted to stay there all night. He could get comfortable in this spot and wake up and the sun would be out. Yeah, he could wait it out.

Either that . . .

Or, deal with the assholes waiting outside.

"Our man's here," Malik said, tapping Donny, behind the steering wheel, on the shoulder and watching Donny's head move forward over the steering wheel to get an angle to see the light coming from a window on the second floor.

Donny fit a pair of black leather gloves, like driving gloves, on his hands and said, "Time to go to work."

Malik watched Donny get out from the front seat and close the driver's side door, one hand on the door handle, guiding it with the other hand to muffle the noise. Waited until Donny was down the alley and out of sight, going through the front of the Casita, before he looked up at the second floor window again, making sure the light was still on.

After that, Malik leaned over the front seat and turned the volume up on the radio, wanting to hear The Manhattans sing "Hurt." He settled back, moving to the music as he did it, almost getting lost in it, but expecting to hear something. Soon. He told Donny to use the suppressor he had for that M9, something an ex-Army guy told him they called the "Hush-Puppy" way back in Vietnam. But still, he thought maybe he'd hear a window breaking or a lamp hitting the floor. Something that told him *something* happened.

Malik just about shit himself when the car door opened.

He couldn't see it. It wasn't in front of him. It was the rear passenger door. Right next to him.

"Evening," the man sliding onto the seat said, a pistol barrel showing in his hand, held tight against his right side.

"You must be Murray."

Murray nodded. "Who are you?"

Malik didn't break his stare.

Murray said, "Tiras Williams send you?"

Again, Malik didn't break his stare.

"Look, you can sit there and say nothing if you want. But, you already said enough. I get in here, first thing you do is say my name. That means you coming to see me," Murray stopped, looking around the interior of the El Dorado, noticing the keys still in the ignition. "Only thing, I don't know you."

Murray waited. Fuck this guy. He wants to sit there, stare, act like a hard-ass. Even with a gun barrel in plain sight.

"Let's go," Murray said, backing up out of the rear passenger door, keeping his eye on the little fucker. Murray moved the .22, motioning for Malik to follow, then closed the door as they stood in the alleyway. Murray looked down the alley past Malik, the street light bouncing off the buildings giving him a good view if anyone was coming, and said, "Your man's going to be coming back soon. You tell him what's going on. You tell him that I have a gun, that he needs to get rid of his. You tell him that or, so help me God, I'll shoot you right here."

"That right?" Malik said, turning to look at Murray.

As soon as Malik stopped talking, Murray heard a noise behind him and turned around, in enough time to see another black man touching the waistband of his pants and hesitating when the white man caught him.

Now, the other hand coming up, palm open, fingers spreading wide. Like he was either trying to calm things down or waiting for the white man to make a move.

Murray said to the second black man, "This your boss?" holding Malik in front of him. He waited for an answer. Maybe the man nodded, maybe not, Murray wasn't sure. Murray said, "What's your name?" Moving the .22 on him to make sure he would get a response. When he heard him say that his name was Donny, Murray said, "Now, Donny, you don't want to do anything dumb . . . So, you take whatever it is tucked under your shirt there and throw it on the ground," and waited while Donny looked at his boss, who nodded his head. Then, Murray told Donny to reach for it with his left hand like he heard guys telling other guys to do it in the movies. Murray told both of them to follow him around to the driver's side while he grabbed the keys from the ignition. He said, "You guys don't have to say anything if you don't want to," keeping the pistol on them while he went for the keys, "but I'm pretty sure Tiras Williams sent you over here." Getting confident.

Murray popped the trunk and could see by the way that the skinny, smaller one was looking at him—head jerked back, eyes bulging—that he couldn't figure out what was going on in Murray's head.

Murray ignored the look and said, "You two climb in," and

kept his gun on them while he said, "make sure you get comfortable in there."

Chapter Twelve

Miranda watched a maroon Buick Park Avenue turn off Northwest Thirty-fourth Street into a parking strip adjacent to Sunshine State Lock and Pawn. She said, "Might be the guest of honor," watching a head in the backseat move up and down like the mouth on it was moving. She saw Reyes pick up the binoculars up to his eyes and read the tag numbers into a radio. A voice came back from the other end before anyone stepped from the Buick, cutting its lights now across the street.

"Registered to his wife, Gertrude," Reyes said.

"He gets a sixty-foot yacht, and she gets a Buick. That's nice."

"She's been dead two years now," Reyes said. "Aortic aneurysm. I heard him talking about it on a tape recording once. Said she'd had the condition for a long time, about ten years."

Miranda took the glasses from Reyes and saw a young, white male with dark features get out from the driver's side of the Buick and walk back up to the street, looking up and down the sidewalk, then bang on the front door. A light came on inside the pawn shop, and the shade on the door went up. Then she watched the young guy go back to the car, open up the back passenger door. Then she saw Caesar Pelli step out.

Miranda said, "That's him."

She handed the binoculars back to Reyes, who said, "Looks smaller than in the photos I've seen." What he was looking at was an elderly man, mid-to-late sixties, full head of brown hair, graying on the sides, in a white and blue windsuit, walking through the front door of Sunshine State Lock and Pawn, while the guy that opened the door locked up after him, pulled down a metal warehouse door that covered the door and front windows, put a heavy padlock on it and disappeared into an alley around the side of the store.

There was a wait, maybe a minute of silence, before Miranda said, "What are you going to do?"

Reyes reached for the backseat, grabbing a bulletproof vest while he said, "We're going to give it a few minutes," slipping it over his head, "see if anybody else shows up."

"That's a good idea," Miranda said, thinking out loud. "Gives time for the merchandise to get there, too."

"If we're lucky," Reyes said, squeezing a Beretta nine between his thighs, "Caesar'll have that diaper on when we bust him."

There was a Ricky, a Bobby, two Tonys, a Sammy and a Steve. But, he liked to go by Stevie, something about having the long *e* sound on the end of his name. Like everybody else.

Caesar turned to face two of them standing in a corner, Ricky and one of the Tonys, and said, "What is this shit?" He was picking at opened boxes sitting on countertops, opening a flap on a couple of them and peeking over it; touching the door on an open locker and giving it half a glance inside; picking a mailing tube off the floor and tossing it in that locker, closing it after. "Clean this up, run a respectable business."

One of the Tonys gave a look to Sammy, his eyes going upward. *Christ, first time the guy shows up in four years, he gets on our ass.* Whatever he thought, Sammy started for the boxes, nodding his head for Tony to help, stacking one on top of the other; moving two at a time, stacking them against a back wall, telling Caesar that he would get to it tomorrow. He waited for a response but didn't get one.

Caesar said, "Is it here?" and waited.

Stevie and the second Tony disappeared into the dark at the back of the store. They disappeared at the same time at first. Then, when Stevie made it to the door of the back office first, he gave the second Tony a look and went in by himself. The second Tony came back and started straightening up, joining everyone else.

"Here it is, boss," Stevie said, coming back with a wooden crate, not a cardboard box, the top fitting loose. "Packaged it real nice even. Straw stuffing and everything."

"They must be doing pretty good down there, those peasants that dig this stuff up," the second Tony said. "You should move down there, go into business, *Steve.*"

That got the second Tony a look from Stevie.

"Knock that shit off," Caesar said, the straw stuffing coming out on the tabletop.

"I got to sit here and take that?" Stevie said, starting to pick up the straw and moving over to a wastebasket.

Caesar said, "Who the fuck asked either of you two anything?"

There was a crowd around the tabletop, guys trying to get a look inside the crate. "You like it?" is what Bobby said when Caesar lifted a piece of gold body armor out of the straw, a ton of it in there, watching the old man's eyes get wide. Caesar looked it over, inspecting some of the smudges and fades.

"Almost two thousand years old," Bobby said.

Okay, he could live with the smudges.

Ricky said, "More where that came from, soon as those *huaqueros* can get to it." When he saw the others' faces, he said, "That's Indian for grave robber, gentlemen."

Ricky waited for a comment from Caesar after he said that, but Caesar ignored it and said, "Turn on the light."

Bobby was closest to the light switch, extending his left arm and moving the toggle up.

It wasn't long after the light came on that Sammy moved to the front door, unsure of whether he had heard something from outside. He raised the shade on the front door and looked through the peep square on the outer warehouse door. He stayed there for a minute and that brought the two Tonys over, three faces crowding into the peep square.

"What is it?" a voice said, Sammy and the two Tonys not sure which.

They didn't turn around, looking through the two by two glass window at a figure, one they could tell was a woman by the shape of a skirt in the light off a street lamp, closing the trunk of a car and starting across Thirty-fourth Street.

As the figure got closer, Sammy said, "Looks like that chick, that Shelly from the club," turning to look at Caesar. "One . . . no, two guys with her . . . they got vests on," sounding like he didn't understand what was happening.

Caesar said, "You sure it's her? Shelly? What would she be doing here?"

Sammy nodded. "Yeah. I wouldn't forget something looked like that."

"That's her," the first Tony said, watching Shelly remove a pistol from a hip holster. "Shit. I wanted to bang her."

They huddled around the Park Avenue. Four of them in bulletproof vests with names of their different organizations on the back of each. Two from the Dade County Sheriff, two from the Miami Beach P.D. Reyes had brought an extra for Miranda. They might be on the Sheriff's Department's turf, but if this bust was going to make the TV news, the good people of Miami were going to know it was the Miami Beach Police Department that was responsible.

"I hope they stay where they are," Reyes said, watching kids running out from shacks across the street, lining up along the chain link fence where their yard met Thirty-fourth. "They hop the fence, that would complicate things." Then, into a radio, talking to officers taking up position on the other side of the building, "Bring it out . . . keep your people there . . . I'm sending two around . . . when it's close, I'll make the call."

As soon as they heard the butane ignite on the torches, Reyes took Miranda and motioned for the two Dade County sheriffs to stay put. Reyes figured his plan was easy: Use torches to cut through the padlock and along the bottom of the warehouse door; the door would roll back into the opening at the top of the storefront; inside, they would see four black SUVs pull up, lights flashing in front of them. They might give some resistance. Try to run. But, there were guys all around the building.

The plan sounded easy. Simple.

But, things have a way of not working out as planned.

Sometimes they turn out easier than you expect.

Caesar had the backflap under his arm. The click of magazines going into pistols was in the background.

"What the hell's going on out there?" Caesar said, his body starting to face the side door.

Sammy was on the balls of his feet, trying to get a view of the base of the front door. "I can't tell," he said, moving his head from left to right then back left. "Wait. I see something . . . like the flash off a blowtorch." Now, the spray from the flame visible. "Man, it's all over the place."

Ricky said, "What are they trying to do, burn us down?" He turned to Caesar. "Boss, you do something to piss this chick off?"

Stevie was the first one out the door. And the first one on the ground. They followed one by one, each of them seeing an open sliding door on a black Chevy Suburban, three Dade County

SWAT team members in full dress pointing MP5 submachine guns at their heads. Two more Suburbans in back of that one. Three guys on the right side of the door. Three guys on the left side of the door.

And one woman.

Caesar didn't say anything, staring at this girl cockeyed. He didn't say anything, but Miranda could see it on his face, in his look. In the pieces of gravel up and down the front of his windsuit.

They were looking at each other when Matt Reyes said, "You quit staring at her. I'm the one you need to worry about." Looking at each other until Miranda watched the Dade County Sheriffs put his hand on Caesar's well-coifed head of brown hair, ducking his head into the back of one of the Suburbans.

Reyes watched the rest of Caesar's crew form a single file line, heads lowered, hands cuffed behind their backs. "What? You thought you could get out the side entrance? That there'd be nobody there? That you'd walk out into the night, get in your vehicles and go home?" Reyes put his face in the last one in line, the second Tony, and said, "You're a bunch of dumb fuckers."

Miranda watched the SWAT guy put his hand on Tony's head, lowering it so he wouldn't bump it getting into the truck. Then, watched Tony fight for space on the backseat next to the others.

She had to get in touch with Jack.

Miranda got back to her car, wondering about how to tell Jack about Caesar. She thought about calling him first, but remembered she didn't have his number. That was okay, it gave her an excuse to see him in person. Yeah, it was news she should tell him in person. Look him in the eye, tell him what happened, and see what happens.

Her cell phone rang. She answered it and heard Harvey Turner's voice on the other end.

"Miranda, I just talked to Bill Cecil. How'd it go tonight?"

"Fine. We've got . . ."

"That's great," Harvey said, cutting Miranda off mid-sentence. "I've already been debriefed on most of it. You can fill in your details in a report tomorrow. What's more pressing is these two men you have staked out in front of a house on, I forget the street name, but somewhere in the Liberty City area."

"I've reassigned them." Before Harvey had a chance to ask where, she said, "To a house on Northwest Twenty-fourth."

"Miranda, we have other obligations and we're short on manpower. And, I don't recall authorizing that. You need to get those guys out of there."

Miranda said he could consider it done and hung up. Before he could ask what they were doing there.

Murray was sleeping it off on a sofa that was too short for him. Still in his jeans and sweatshirt, tennis shoes hanging over the wicker armrest on the end of the sofa. Wondering if he should still be here after everything that had gone on tonight.

Murray popped up with a knock on the door. He looked at the digital clock on the microwave. Ten-thirty at night. Shit, who the hell was this? He felt for the .22 in the pocket of his sweatshirt, figuring he should be sleeping with it anyway. He had his hand on it, keeping it in the pocket, while he asked who it was through the door.

The voice on the other side said, "It's Miranda."

Murray opened the door, and she said, "It's late. I'm sorry, but I needed to talk to you," before he could get anything out.

He let her in and shrugged it off. Hey, he was happy it wasn't something else. An FBI agent at his door at ten-thirty at night was okay, considering.

Murray said, "What's going on?"

"I just wanted to talk to you about some things that went down tonight. I didn't have your number . . ."

"The FBI couldn't get that for you?"

She smiled. "So, I came over." With a smile on her face.

Murray looked at her. She had on another skirt. A different one, blue this time. Looking good, even with a glisten of sweat on her brow.

He said, "You want to get a drink?"

Chapter Thirteen

What Chuco was supposed to do was park in front of the house, honk the horn, get in his Buick and drive off.

But, man, he liked this El Dorado. Thinking about what he could do with it. Spending the whole drive over here from Jack Murray's place looking at the dashboard, imagining a mounted DVD player or GPS. It would be perfect for a custom grille insert. Yeah, that would look gooood. Even a cat-back exhaust that he could show off at the races on Rickenbacker Causeway.

Headlights came up on the side of Chuco as he pulled up in front of the house that Jack Murray told him about. Ernesto, one of his boys, followed in the Buick. Chuco watched Ernesto's arm, skinny in the dashboard light, reach across to roll the passenger window down and heard him say, "I wanna get out of here, man."

Chuco said, "Hang on a minute," half his attention on Ernesto, half on the banging coming from inside the trunk. Man, cuss words he never heard of coming from there. "I want to get this car."

"Man, you fucking crazy," Ernesto said. "These guys are crazy. They'll kill us."

"Gimme that stick under your seat."

Ernesto reached under the driver's side seat, feeling for the stick, then looking down, getting serious about it after Chuco told him to hurry up. Handing the foot-and-a-half long smoothed out piece of wood to Chuco, Ernesto said, "They start making trouble, you best get in here fast. Else I'm leaving."

Chuco crept up to the trunk of the El Dorado, stepping light, in a crouched position like he was waiting for it to bust open. He stayed to the side of it, his body against the rear quarter panel and banged on the top of it with his stick.

"I'm going to let you out, okay? Now, you going to be nice and walk away, inside your friend's house. Okay?"

"Fuck you, motherfucker," a voice said, muffled through the sheet metal.

"Okay, that's not nice." Chuco took a moment to look at Ernesto, who told Chuco to hurry this shit up. "My friend has a gun. You give some trouble, he's going to shoot you between the eyes."

"What the fuck is going on here?"

It was a voice from the driveway.

Chuco jumped at the sound of it, seeing a figure—a big, black one, pump action shotgun in hand—backlit against lights coming through a living room window.

Chuco settled for a second before saying, "Ain't nothing going on here, man." Then, turned for his Buick sitting in the middle of the street, at the same time wondering why he didn't hear Ernesto starting to gun it, and saw two other figures against the Buick's front bumper. One of them, a big, fat one, walked around the driver's side and yanked Ernesto out by his shirt collar. Barely giving him time to put the car in park.

"Nothing going on, huh?" Tiras Williams circled the white El Dorado. He knew the car. Giving a look to that little shit with a club in his hand while he did it. Meaning it, too. Tiras stopped, hearing a voice yell his name from the trunk.

Tiras said, "Give me the keys," raising his voice.

Chuco turned, whipping around, when one of the guys behind him grabbed the club from his hand.

Tiras put the key in, hearing his name a couple more times as he did it, and opened the lid. The inside light went on, and there was Malik and some guy, he didn't know the name, hunched together, mean looks on their faces turning to joy.

Malik moved his body to see over the lip of the trunk. "Where we at?"

Tiras said, "You're at my house."

Malik was out first, pushing off the inside wall and twisting, tripping as he got out to the street. Tiras didn't watch the other one get out. He was busy holding Malik back, Tiras calming him down when he saw lights start to go on in front room windows around him. Tiras had his body straight up, tense, his hands on Malik's forearms, holding them down at Malik's sides.

When he thought Malik was under control, Malik just rubbernecking to see around Tiras, to see who it was driving his car, Tiras said, "Not out here. Go on inside and settle down." Tiras let go and told Kwame to toss him the club. "Take this inside with you, but it ain't for fucking my house up," he said, handing it to Malik. "You get the chance to use it later."

Tiras looked at Malik, making sure Malik did what he told him to do. Tiras watched him walk down the driveway, up the front stoop, and through the front door. Tiras moved toward the, what was he, a Mexican? Could be. Or maybe something else. They had so many different ones down here from that general part of the world. Shoot, he had done business with Guatemalans, Chileans, Bolivians, a few others. Just to say. Some of the Colombians were good friends of his. He half-circled the Mexican, deciding that's what he was after hearing his accent. Walking half-circles back and forth in front of him. Pacing, giving this guy a look to put a scare into him.

"What's your name, man?"

"Rafael."

Tiras kept giving the look. Intimidate this Rafael into just telling him what he wanted to know, so he wouldn't have to ask questions. Go through all that trouble. Shit, he got himself surrounded by a bunch of mean-looking brothers, one of them in front of him with a shotgun. Guy should be talking.

Tiras waited until he got tired of it and said, "What you doing in front of my house with these two in the trunk of that car?"

"I was told to drop them off here."

"And why didn't you just do that?" Tiras watched the stupid look on Rafael's face and decided he didn't want to wait for the answer to that one. So, he said, "Who told you to do that?"

Rafael hesitated.

"Look," Tiras rested the shotgun barrel against his shoulder, "you answer my questions, you get out of here okay."

Maybe.

"My friend told me to do that."

Tiras nodded his head and looked around, in all directions. Getting pissed. "Who your friend?" When Rafael didn't answer right away, Tiras's gaze moved from the Mexican in front of him to Lil' Man, then to Kwame and the other guy in the trunk with Malik, standing in back of the other Mexican, the one driving that big old-time car. "You don't wanna talk out here, maybe you uncomfortable," he said, looking at Rafael again. "C'mon. You'll feel better inside."

Inside, Rudy, walking back into the living room from the kitchen, saw them file past him, in a straight line down a narrow hallway. Into a room somewhere in the back of the house. He recognized Chuco, and they looked each other in the eye, each caught off guard seeing the other there. Tiras was last in line. He stopped when he saw Rudy, letting the others keep going.

Rudy poked his head in the hall and watched Kwame open a door back there, like a doorman, the others going in. Chuco and another Mexican shoved in. He tried to get some answers while Tiras was talking to Kwame, yelling down the hall, giving instructions on what to do, finishing with, "Make sure he talk to you."

Rudy said, "What are they doing here?"

Tiras yelled out Kwame's name a couple times before the door opened and Kwame's head popped out. Then, yelling some more, telling Kwame what he wanted them to do, how he wanted it done.

Rudy was ready when Tiras turned back to him, giving him his full attention with hands cupped in front of his body.

Only thing now was that Rudy's train of thought was broken by sounds coming from the back of the house.

"Now, what you want."

A loud whooshing sound.

"What are they doing here?"

The crack of one object slamming into another.

"Why you need to know that?"

Screaming.

"I know one of those guys."

Tiras's eyes got big. Surprised by this piece of information. "Which one?"

"He was the first one in line. His name's Rafael."

Tiras nodded. "I met Rafael outside. Me and him's good friends now."

More screams.

"Just like you my friend, Rudy."

Tiras smiled.

Great. What was that about? Rudy wondered if he should just stop talking.

Tiras said, "Tell me how you know this guy," and moved Rudy to the living room.

"The one guy, Rafael, he's a stoner. We worked together

sometimes, long time ago."

As soon as he said it, Rudy could tell what was coming next.

"I guess this guy know Jack Murray, too."

"Why would you think that?"

"Because a couple of them boys in that room with your friend, I sent them over to Jack Murray's house tonight. They come back to me, not with news that my five thousand dollars was well spent. Not with good news. They come back to me in the trunk of a car, cuddled up nut-to-butt like a couple faggots."

Oh.

Rudy didn't say anything, didn't know what to say to that, until the sound of a door opening got both of them looking up. Footsteps coming down the hall until Kwame appeared in the living room. Jeez, sweating heavy.

"I don't think they can take no more, chief," Kwame said. "Shoot, even I wore out." Bringing his shirt up to wipe his forehead.

"Go on ahead," Tiras said. "I'll be in di-rectly."

Rudy grabbed Tiras by the arm before he could disappear into the hallway and said, "What the hell're you going to do?"

"We going to send Jack Murray one more message."

Murray and Miranda were at Mac's Club Deuce. Mostly because it was close, a half-block down from the Casita. Murray liked it because it was cheap, relatively speaking. Miranda liked that they could get a table and that it was dark. She thought she looked like shit.

Murray checked his pocket as they sat down, trying to do it without Miranda noticing. Enough there for a couple of rounds, but he wished they'd done this a few hours earlier, enough time to make the eleven-hour happy hour.

Miranda looked like she did the last time she showed up at

his door. Nervous. Murray made small talk on the way over, letting them sit down and get comfortable before he said, "So, what's the emergency?"

He wondered how that sounded.

Miranda sipped, taking a moment, and said, "Jack, what are your plans for the future?"

Murray didn't know that he had any specific plans. Or, that he had any to talk about at a moment's notice. He thought it was a little much to talk about sitting around drinking a beer.

After thinking about it, stalling, Murray shrugged.

"You have any prospects for a job, outside of what you're doing now?"

Sounding serious.

It caught Murray off guard. The tone of the whole conversation. He didn't expect it or come armed with anything he thought he should say. So, he was sure his surprise sounded genuine when all he said was, "Not really." Then, his tone sharper when he said, "What's going on?"

"I'm asking you these questions because I picked up your employer tonight for trafficking in illicit contraband, and I think these are things you need to start thinking about."

Murray said, "What kind of contraband?" almost to make sure he heard it right.

Miranda looking him in the eye when she said, "Caesar was picked up by a combined federal and local task force for smuggling ancient Indian artifacts from Peru."

Murray wasn't familiar with how steep a crime that was, not being too familiar with ancient Indian artifacts. Matter of fact, he was surprised to hear that Caesar was.

"It's a pretty serious offense," Miranda said. "Something the Bureau started cracking down on in the nineties. In the last few years, some of the focus has come off. But, somebody somewhere convinced *his* boss that these items are being resold, in this country, and that money may be going to some terror cell . . ."

"You serious? That Caesar's helping out the terrorists?"

That was a stretch.

She knew it and said, "I'm not, but somebody is," to make her point. "Regardless, he could be looking at some serious time. Even if there's some leniency, which I doubt because this is going to federal court. Considering his advanced age, it'll probably be for the rest of his life."

That last part—the rest of his life—made Murray sad. He watched Miranda sip her beer and put the bottle down, holding it by the neck. He could tell by her look that his answers to her questions weren't working. So, he decided to tell her, "I've always wanted to run a charter fishing service."

Make the trip worth her while.

That surprised her, and she looked at him a moment before saying, "Really?"

Murray nodded.

"How come you never mentioned it before?"

Murray leaned back in his chair and said, "It's not something I talk about much to anyone. You start talking about a thirty-foot fishing boat, two hundred horsepower outboard engine, insurance, licensing, all that costs a lot of money. I never had much luck with money."

She said, "What you've been doing, the pay's not good enough for you to put some away," seeming interested.

"Never seems to be enough to go around." Murray left it there, starting to get uneasy just talking about it. "What about you? You ever think of doing anything else?"

"What else would I do?"

Murray said, "Well, you may have a future as an exotic dancer," and waited to see if that got a smile.

It did.

"God, I was awful," Miranda said, shaking her head.

"How about your degree?" You said something about psychology the first time we met . . ."

He just made one point, remembering when they met. He could see it in her face.

"Was that for real?" he said.

Miranda shook her head. "That was my cover. Got my B.A. in criminal justice at Central Florida. Got my J.D. at Miami after that."

"So, you're a lawyer?"

"I've never practiced. I visited with an FBI recruiter when I was an undergrad and stayed in touch with him. Then, stayed in touch with his replacement. I mean, I'm not going to leave this to work at a firm. I don't care what the pay is."

"If you don't mind my asking, how old are you?"

Able to ask something like that because he was dealing with a mature woman. That was the feeling he got.

Miranda said, "Thirty-two."

"I thought you were *twenty*-two, maybe twenty-three."

Another point.

Feeling a comfort level now, Murray said, "Let me ask you, now that I know you're a lawyer. What are Caesar's chances?"

"Not good. By the letter of the law, this is a serious crime. What makes it worse is that the Bureau has a lot of leeway right now and my boss is looking to make a name. Unfortunately, he's going to use your boss to do that."

"And he's going to try and make this look like some terrorist thing, like you said earlier?"

"He may. You mention words like 'Peru' and 'smuggling' in the paper, with all the insurgency problems they've had down there with the Shining Path and all that. The average American will probably think that it has something to do with terrorism and the Bureau can use that. He could hold Caesar as a person of interest. Either that, or it gets tied up in federal court."

"Basically, he's fucked."

"Basically, yes."

The waitress came with another round and asked Murray if they needed anything else. Miranda watched him tell the waitress no, that they were okay and help her with the empty bottles.

"Anything happening on this thing with Tiras Williams?"

She could tell by his reaction that he wasn't sure about the question.

"Are you asking me or advising me?"

She thought that was cute and laughed. "I'm asking you."

"Miranda," Murray said, "you may know more about that than I do."

"So you've dropped it?"

"I'm strongly considering it."

Miranda said, "I think that's a good idea," and sipped her beer. "Nothing good can come from that."

"I'm glad to hear you approve." Murray was happy the way he handled the situation. Maybe he was considering dropping it. At this point, he wasn't sure. He said, "What do you propose I do with myself?"

"How about a job?"

Murray sat back and thought about it. He couldn't remember ever having what he would call a normal-type job. "There's not a lot of call for the kinds of skills I have."

Miranda shrugged, looking at the bottle. "There's people out there with less skills than you that do well for themselves."

"I think about people that are successful in life, people doing something constructive, I think about someone like you."

Another point, maybe.

Murray smiled, liking the way this was going. "Look, you're

obviously an intelligent woman that's good at what she does. I'm unemployed with very few prospects for a future." He hunched over the table. "Where does that leave us?"

They were on Murray's sofa, the wicker one, Murray wondering if she was comfortable. This was turning out way better than he expected. He was surprised when she said, "How about your place?" to his where-does-that-leave-us remark. "How about your place?" Feeling like he was twenty-years-old again.

Murray was playing it over in his mind until Miranda said, "Come with me," and took him by the hand. They started kissing, standing next to the bed, getting into it before Miranda grabbed Murray's t-shirt and pulled it over his head and off. He thought about what he looked like to her, in the street light filtering through the blinds. He knew he wasn't in great shape. But, rangy, with the kind of tone in his body that came naturally. She bit her bottom lip and ran her fingers along his stomach. Not ripped but flat. He watched her undress, Miranda down to her bra and panties before Murray kicked his shoes off, laces still tied. He was unzipping his jeans as Miranda sat on the edge of his bed, crossing her legs. He watched her looking like the poster inside a World War Two soldier's footlocker and noticed, my God, her body. Not sure if he had ever seen a naked woman with a body like that before. Probably not. Got his jeans and socks off and climbed on top of her.

She said his name a couple of times, and he asked her if she was okay. She said yeah, then, "I can't believe we're doing this." Smiling as she said it.

That was a good sign.

Their bodies intertwined on the bed, kissing, touching, feeling each other. Murray had his hands on Miranda's hip, running it up and down the side of her torso. Looking at her while he was doing it, this was everything he imagined it might be.

She started saying his name again, but in a different tone of voice. This time, Murray didn't ask any questions.

Faye Russo watched from her kitchen window; watched Rudy Maxa trying to get a leg up onto the window unit air conditioner so he could use it to climb into her house, through one of the living room windows. She had seen this before, mostly when he was drunk. Too drunk to remember he had a key or where she kept the spare. He didn't look drunk to her this time, just like a fool trying to get his leg up on the angle bar that held the unit up to the side of the house.

She had the card that nice lady officer gave her, feeling it between her fingers in the pocket of her robe right now. She could call, *should* call; she said she wasn't interested in Rudy. But, she didn't want to get Jack Murray in trouble, either. Maybe she could get Rudy away from that asshole Tiras Williams, though. She said something about that.

Okay, give her a call and go around, let Rudy in before he hurts himself. Well, how about let Rudy in then call the lady officer after. See if he has some cigarettes and grocery money first.

Miranda woke up with the sound of her phone vibrating. Something she had been patterned to hear by now, no matter how much clothes were buried on top of it. She looked at the number but didn't recognize it.

She stepped lightly into the next room, opened the phone, said hello, and waited while the voice on the other end said, "Ma'am, this is Faye Russo. You remember me?"

"Yes, I do, Faye. What can I do for you?"

Faye said, "Ma'am, Rudy is here right now. He don't know I'm talking to you."

Miranda thought, at first, about asking Faye to stop calling her "ma'am." Instead, she said, "How long has he been there?"

"He just got here."

Miranda sat on the edge of the coffee table and said in a whisper, "I'll be there soon," looking over her shoulder toward the bedroom door. "Call me at this number if he leaves." She hung up and went back into the bedroom, trying not to wake Jack up.

Chapter Fourteen

Rudy got pissed when Faye told him that she had called Miranda. She told Rudy that the lady officer could help him, that she was real important-looking. With an important-looking business title on her business card. Look, it said *Miranda Mendoza, Special Agent, Federal Bureau of Investigation.*

Rudy shook his head when Faye tried to show him the card. Holding it out in front of him, Rudy waved it off, taking a swipe at it, and sat back in his chair. That dirty bitch, squealing to that woman that dragged me down the street. I tell you that, Faye? She practically took my arm off. Thinking she was being cute, trying to get her point across. There was a knock at the door. Rudy stayed seated while Faye got up. As she opened it, Rudy saw Miranda's figure through the grillwork on the front of the screen door. He watched Faye let her in, not saying anything to Miranda, both of them looking at him. Like some fucking drug intervention.

Miranda sat on the edge of the seat catty-corner to Rudy's and he said, "What do you want?"

She said, "Things not going so good, are they?" playing off the tone in his voice.

"They were until you got here."

"Is that right?" Miranda said. "Is that why Faye called me, tells me you're climbing onto the air conditioner, trying to get inside her house in the middle of the night. That's what you consider fine?"

Rudy looked past Miranda to Faye. "I didn't want to wake you up, that's all."

Miranda said Rudy's name and that brought his attention back to her. She said, "I'm going to be your friend right now, okay?" and watched his face. "As your friend, I'm telling you that your situation is hopeless."

"That's what you call being a friend?"

Faye said, "Listen to her, Rudy."

"Look," Miranda said, "whatever deal you and Tiras Williams are into, it's not going to go well. We've talked about this before."

"Yeah, I remember."

"Was Jack Murray with you?"

"When?"

"Through any of this."

"This is not his deal. I told you that. Him and Tiras have been going back and forth, though. Childish bullshit."

"What're you talking about?"

"Like tonight, I guess Tiras sent a couple of guys over to Jack's house. Jack turned it around on him, and they ended up back at Tiras's house in the back of some car. They been doing that kind of stuff the past couple of days. It's unprofessional, really."

"Whose car?"

"I don't know whose car. But, the guy that dropped them off, his name is Rafael Rojas. He's a guy that both me and Jack have worked with before."

"This was *tonight?*"

"Right before I came over here. They left, so I left."

"Where do you suppose they are now?"

"Who knows?"

"Could they be going back to Murray's?"

"Maybe. Tiras said he was going to send him a message."

"That's all he said? Send him a message?"

Rudy nodded.

Miranda said, "You think your friends might come over here?"

"They're not my friends, man. I don't know what they are. They scare the shit out of me." Rudy lowered his head and ran his hands through his hair. "I guess that doesn't matter anymore anyhow."

"What do you mean?"

Rudy said, "Assholes," shaking his head.

"Rudy, what's going on?"

"That deal you were talking about," Rudy said. "I was supposed to be in. It was *my* fucking deal, for chrissakes."

"You're out now?"

"I will be. As soon as my contact comes in from Atlanta."

"Is he here now?"

"Tomorrow, maybe. Possibly day after."

"You talked to him?"

Rudy nodded. "Yesterday."

"Where're they meeting?"

"Didn't say."

"Maybe at Tiras's house?"

"I'm not saying another fucking word. You come over here, asking me questions that're gonna get me killed."

"Rudy, you stay with that crew, and you're as good as dead. Now, you come over here, and you put Faye in danger. Wherever those guys are, they're going to come back and they're going to wonder where you are. Eventually, they'll find their way over here."

Faye said, "Yeah. And, they make such a mess of my living room when they come over."

Murray woke up, not right away, his eyes taking time to adjust to early morning sunlight coming through his bedroom window. The way he woke up, he was on his side facing the wall. He turned his body enough to reach over to her. She wasn't there. Murray didn't move right away. Maybe she was in the bathroom, one of those women that always woke up to go to the bathroom, even at thirty-two. He looked over and saw the door was open and he didn't hear any noise coming from there.

He took his time getting out of bed. Not that he really wanted to, especially after seeing that it wasn't even six-thirty in the morning by the clock on the microwave. He looked for a note, thinking she might have left one. Nothing. That would have been nice, at least to let him know where she had gone off to. He thought things had gone well. Maybe she didn't. He remembered her saying, "I can't believe we're doing this." But, smiling when she said it. All that, now he had to worry about whether or not he'd hear from her again.

Murray made it over to the kitchen, still groggy. He blinked his eyes a few times, trying to loosen the sleep from around the corners, and opened the shade facing out to the alley. He looked down and saw Chuco's Buick parked there. Dents all over the outside like somebody took a baseball bat to it.

Something else to worry about.

Gina ran back down the driveway, no bra, tits bouncing under her tank top, and handed the newspaper to Nicky Silva. She pointed to headline, front page, above the fold, right under the *Sun-Sentinel* logo:

LOCAL ORGANIZED CRIME FIGURE ARRESTED

Nicky was quiet when he read it, having to hold his hand up for Gina to stop talking. Nicky read aloud about a joint task force, the eight-month investigation and ancient artifacts from Peru. He got silent again when he read the comments from Harvey Turner, someone the paper called "local FBI bureau chief," moving his lips along with the words. Nicky followed the lines with his index finger while the local FBI bureau chief talked about putting Caesar away for good "to ensure that this type of wanton apathy for the law doesn't happen again." Nicky read the word "wanton" over again but he didn't recognize it, except maybe as some soup he had at a Chinese restaurant one time. That's how he decided it was pronounced and moved on.

He threw the paper aside and made some calls. First to Tony. Then to Bobby. No answer either place. He tried Stevie's cell phone. He figured he had better stop. Maybe the feds already have a trap on those lines. Maybe they could trace the phone number back to him. They did things like that. Especially the cell phone. It was a dumb move. He thought about who else to call when he heard Gina say, "Whaddya think's gonna happen?" before he knew she had enough time to finish the article. He looked over at her, all tits and hair first thing in the morning, and said, "Why don't you finish the whole thing before asking me stupid fucking questions?"

Truth is, he didn't know what was going to happen. He should've been there except he got sent on that thing with Jack Murray. He could pray to Saint Rosalia later for that.

Gina kept at it with questions. Like, "What're you gonna do?"

"I'm not sure."

"You weren't able to talk to nobody?"

"Did you hear me talking to anybody? Get your head out of your ass."

Gina said, "Fuck you," and disappeared into the bathroom.

Nicky said, "You're just worried about who's gonna pay for your next manicure," and heard the door slam.

Shit, at least it gave him time to think. Maybe there were some guys that weren't at the shop last night that didn't get busted. He could try giving somebody else a call. Only he didn't know if somebody was already watching them. The guys back in

Bensonhurst? They didn't have anything going on. That's why he pushed to come down here, bugging the boss so much that Nicky thought they were going to take *him* out back one night. To be an earner. Somebody from there would probably be calling soon anyway. What else?

Hey, Jack Murray wasn't there either, and he had something going on.

The way Miranda worked it, she let Rudy and Faye leave, go anywhere they wanted to. Get as far away as they could and got them started with some gas money. How far would they get? She didn't know, but if Rudy was as scared as he said, they'd be smart to go as far as possible and not worry about it. She waited around after they left, parked across the street in case Tiras Williams came around. An hour passed before she decided to drive by Jack Murray's to see what was up there. She walked up the alley, all the way up to an old beat up car and looked up at his window. It was dark, like she left it. After that, back to her apartment for a couple hours of sleep before going to the office.

She passed Harvey Turner in the hallway. They stopped to talk for a minute, mostly chit-chat about the Caesar Pelli bust. It was all stuff they had been over before, and Harvey didn't seem too interested in any details she might have wanted to add right then. He was probably tired from doing press conferences and giving interviews last night so the newspapers and TV news could have something this morning. Which was okay by her, she wasn't in the mood for him anyway.

Harvey had come and gone without asking any more questions about the two agents they talked about before. And she didn't tell him.

"Looks like you had some company," Nicky Silva said, holding up a compact for Murray to see. "Looks like an expensive one," he said, flipping it over. "Nice."

Murray passed him, bringing junk to the kitchen garbage can. "You know a lot about women's cosmetics, do you?"

Nicky said that, yeah, he knew something about it. Hey, he pays attention and that chicks eat that shit up, and that he's had a lot of chicks, and he's seen some different kinds. Enough to know that this one wasn't top of the line, but certainly upper-middle class.

Murray forgot what a ladies' man he was talking to. Hard to do since Nicky liked to remind him of it, like when he said to Murray, "You do her like I told you? You do some of the things I told you about? I bet you did, didn't even give me credit, huh?"

"Credit for what?"

"My move. Or one of the moves I showed you."

"You want me to stop in the middle of everything and say 'Hey, you remember that guy Nick I introduced you to the other day? This is a move he showed me.' "

"So it was that chick from the other day, huh? She's good looking, man. I'd hit that, too."

Murray was tying the handles on a garbage bag, ready to take it outside, when he said, "What are you doing here anyway?"

"I guess you saw the paper this morning. The thing with Caesar."

Murray nodded, making it a point to pick up a copy of the *Herald* after he dropped Chuco's car in a lot over on 13th.

Nicky said, "What you think about that?"

"I think Caesar got careless and it cost him. I mean, he didn't have to be there. And it's going to cost everybody. I know I'm screwed. The only reason I have this place is because of him. Same thing with my job. Come the first of the month, I'm not sure where I'm going to be."

"So you got nothing going on?"

Murray felt it coming and left with his trash bag without answering the question. Walking to the Dumpster out back, he weighed it in his mind. He had already decided that he was going to see Tiras, try to reason with the guy, man to man, instead of carrying on like this. Maybe Tiras would take to it, maybe not. But, when he saw the old Buick all beat to shit and no Chuco inside, he figured the back and forth had to stop. After last night, he wasn't sure what he had left to lose anyway. Miranda went through his mind right then. He wasn't sure what they had, maybe just that one night. That wouldn't pay the bills, though.

On his way back to the apartment now, Murray decided he could use the help. Especially if he was going to meet Tiras on his own turf.

He walked in, closed the door, and said, "I got something I can maybe use your help on."

Nicky Silva didn't say anything right away. Just sat down, fluffing the crease in his trousers as he did it, and watched Murray put another trash can liner in before he said, "This have to do with those same jigs from the other night?"

"Yes, it does."

Nicky said, "I knew it," and smiled like he was old friends with Murray. "I said to myself, that Jack, he's a player. He's got these couple niggers to take care of, move on to bigger and better business."

"Look, when we see them, try to watch it with the racial stuff, okay. They probably know what they are. They don't need you to remind them, alright?"

Nicky nodded and said, "I'll remember that." He watched Murray picking up things, cleaning up around him and said, "When is this going down?"

"I'm hoping to meet this afternoon. Why don't you go home, get slicked up, come back and we'll go over there."

"What happens then?"

Murray said, "Well, I'm not sure about that. I want to meet with these people, straighten things out. Come to some kind of understanding. We'll see where it goes from there." He looked up at Nicky. "Still interested?" Nicky nodded and Murray said, "Any deal I get, you get ten percent. How's that?"

No fucking way that's all I'm getting, Nicky thought to himself. He said to Murray, "Sounds good."

Harvey's voice was flat when he said, "I spoke with the two agents we discussed last night." Then, adding a tone of surprise when he said, "They told me you had them watching some drug dealer's house in the Liberty City area. You care to tell me about that?"

Not really, Miranda thought. She said, "I'm sorry we didn't talk about it before. Everyone was so busy with the investigation. I never had a chance to touch base with you."

"Well, I'm glad we have time now. Time to sit down and talk about how things are going," Harvey said. "Get to know each other a little better."

Miranda wondered what that meant and said, "The house they were watching belongs to Tiras Williams."

"Tiras Williams? I don't recognize the name."

"I didn't either until I did some research. Turns out he's into a lot of bad stuff. Drugs for starters. Guns. He's stayed clean so far, but his name did come up in the statement of a Guatemalan national picked up by Metro-Dade two years ago on a drug buy."

"Is there any connection to the Pelli organization?"

"I had to yank those guys before I could determine that." Miranda almost smiled at the thought of sticking Harvey with that one, watching his jaw stiffen. "He would arrange meets at the club. Sometimes with guys who were known associates of

Caesar, sometimes with others."

"Who were the others?"

"The only one I got an i.d. on was a guy named Rudy Maxa. He's from the same neighborhood."

"Two guys from Liberty City coming all the way out to the Beach to talk business? Sounds like there could be something there."

"That's what I'm saying. It suggested the possibility that they were doing business with Caesar or somebody under him. Or, that they were acting as intermediaries."

"Or, they just like watching titty shows," Harvey said.

"They could do that in their own neck of the woods."

Harvey said, "The second guy, Rudy Maxa . . . Where's he now?"

"Disappeared."

"That would make an investigation somewhat difficult, wouldn't it?"

"Not if we still have Tiras. And, you can bet he's the key figure here."

"The key to what? Look, there's nothing I love better than the Patriot Act, but you saying 'you can bet' is like telling me you don't know what's going on."

"Harvey, I know I screwed up before. I'm holding myself accountable for that. It was a hunch. But, I still have that hunch. It'll probably end up that Tiras isn't connected to one of Caesar Pelli's guys . . ."

"It'd be hard to do business with anyone in Caesar's group anyway. They didn't move without his say-so, and he's in a holding cell right now. *Incommunicado.*"

"That's a great point," Miranda said. "But, my hunch is that we can get a new investigation going on Tiras Williams. I'll bet he's got some big deals going right now."

"There you go using that word 'bet' again."

"C'mon, Harvey," Miranda said, thinking she might be pushing too hard. Then, let it go and said, "We'll bust this guy and make great copy for the Bureau. You can see the lead paragraph, 'Fresh off the arrest of crime lord Caesar Pelli . . .' "

Harvey Turner leaned back, resting his chin on his closed fist. "We'll give it a go. But you're going to have to run things through me."

"So you'll let me set it up?"

"You can run it on the ground so long as you understand I'm supervising you. Your leash isn't tight, but it's going to be short for a while."

"I do and I'll get everything started today."

"You do that," Harvey said. "And, Miranda, why don't we talk about the rest over dinner this evening?"

"I don't know what else we would have to discuss." That's what Miranda thought she should have said. Or, how about "I'll already be up and running by tonight." Stick it to him. She *did* plan to be up and running by tonight. This afternoon, if she could swing it. She would put the wheels in motion after a phone call to find out about Special Agents Phelps (it made her think of old *Mission: Impossible* reruns she would watch with her dad) and Taylor, the two agents she had requisitioned before. They were familiar with the area and probably weren't doing anything special for anybody special.

Instead, she hadn't said anything, just nodded at Harvey and would have to screen calls all day to make sure he wasn't going to take her up on it.

"Bill?" Miranda said.

"I heard you had a spot of trouble."

"Nothing I couldn't talk my way out of."

"That's tough to do with Harvey. Even if you catch him in a moment of weakness, which is rare."

"Not that hard if you play to his ego." She heard Bill laughing on the other end of the line and then said, "I need a favor."

"Shoot."

"Could you contact Personnel and find out what Special Agents Phelps and Taylor are assigned to?"

"You can do that."

"Yeah, but I can't yank them off whatever they're doing."

"Oh," Bill Cecil said. "And, why do I want to yank them off what they're doing?"

"So they can join a detail I'm putting together."

"I'm impressed."

"I'm surprised."

"Well, I didn't want to be the one to say it. What, exactly, is this detail?"

"We're going to be investigating a young drug dealer named Tiras Williams. Starting with surveillance, and that's why I need these two."

"Why these two in particular?"

"Because this is the same thing they were doing for me yesterday."

"I guess you hadn't run that one by Harvey."

"No," Miranda said, "and now I need to backtrack and go through him."

"How'd you stumble on Tiras Williams in the first place?"

"He'd pop into the club with his associates every now and then. I did some research, tried to pitch it to Harvey as an ancillary to his Caesar Pelli investigation. I don't know how well that worked, but it worked well enough to get me this."

"He ever come in to meet with Jack Murray?"

"You remembered his name."

"Of course I did. You're practically my surrogate daughter . . . So?"

"They did have a mutual acquaintance."

"What's his name?"

"Rudy Maxa. He used to work with Jack. But after Jack went away on a robbery charge, he ended up with Tiras. I guess there have been some problems."

"Let me ask you this," Bill Cecil said. "What if your investigation leads back to your boyfriend? What happens then?"

Murray was getting restless waiting on Nicky Silva. Probably a mistake to let him go home and get ready. What Murray meant was to go home, get your gun, get two or three guns, get a loose pair of jeans that you could hide them in easily, and come back. He could picture Nicky ironing a pair of slacks and putting gel in his hair. Maybe shaving. It gave him a thought to call the whole thing off. Just pack up his stuff, go get Chuco's Buick and drive off.

He settled down and started to get ready, telling himself that he was just going to meet with Tiras. That was it, just talk. Come to an understanding, like he told Nicky. If it didn't work, walk out, give Nicky an excuse to go home, and then drive off. If it didn't work, at least he *hoped* to get the chance to walk out of there. Getting out of there without a mess, that was the hard part.

It didn't take long for Bill Cecil to call with news. The agents Miranda wanted were about to be reassigned to her, pulled off what they were doing, that her operation was a priority. She was sure he made it sound good to whoever was in charge of what investigation Phelps and Taylor were on. But, he didn't really have to. Bill had enough authority that people just listened. He was a good friend to have. But, he had a sometimes annoying habit of being reasonable. Like what he said about Jack. What if the investigation ends up involving him? On one hand, she couldn't see it happening. Tiras and his crew were not Jack's kind of guys. Not the kind that she could see him trusting with any of his business anyway. On the other hand, Jack was stuck. She remembered him talking about running a commercial charter. But, being realistic about it, knowing that it took money and time to do something like that. He made it sound like a long shot. She wondered if Jack was the kind of guy that went after a long shot. Or, did he like the sure thing, something he could see right in front of him?

Seven-thirty in the morning, still dark out, a navy blue Suburban turned onto Northwest Fourth and crept along, looking for the little shotgun house with faded blue shutters and peeling paint. Passed it up at first, found it, backed up. A figure appeared as the driver's door opened, walking across the street and up steps to the front door. All the lights off inside. Several quick knocks on the door, getting louder with each round. A few minutes passed before there was a honk and the man turned back for the street.

"Nobody home," he said to another man sitting in the passenger seat across the center console.

"How you like that?" Lloyd Bone said. "He call me, I come all this way and he ain't even here."

Chapter Fifteen

Tiras would get up from the kitchen table and walk around, pacing back and forth on the linoleum, screaming about what he was going to do to Rudy if he ever found him. Yelling, "Can you believe that motherfucker? That little sack of shit?" to no one in particular, although Lil' Man was close enough to hear, sitting at the kitchen table just listening. "I'm close to the biggest deal of my life, and this motherfucker is nowhere to be found," Tiras said to him. "Fucking gone."

It kind of annoyed Lil' Man that he had gotten stuck here, having to listen to Tiras going on and on about it. Okay, he was gone. We find that little shit, we gonna smoke him. But, shit, we still here. Kwame and me, we gonna back you up. Rudy wouldn't be good for that kind of thing anyway. Can't stand the sight of blood. Plus, it was, like, five hours ago when we went by his house. Tiras was still talking about it. Rudy had already made the call. Tiras could deal with the man directly.

What good was Rudy now anyway?

Lil' Man listened out of one ear, nodding when he thought he had to or felt Tiras looking at him and looked past the foyer out into the living room at Kwame. That was annoying, too. Kwame getting up and walking out when he felt the shit starting to hit the fan. Kwame in there doping on meth leaving Lil' Man to do the listening. Kwame was the one hopped up, bouncing around in an easy chair, talking a hundred miles an hour. Shit, him and Tiras, they could've talked each other's ear off.

Lil' Man got up, thinking about a peanut butter and fried banana sandwich. He heard that that's what Elvis liked. Not that he liked Elvis or listened to his music. Some of it was okay, though. He had listened to it before, a few times from his momma's record collection. Enough to convince him that the man had some black in his family tree somewhere along the line. No, it was just that he liked the idea of peanut butter and fried bananas together and taught himself how to make it. No wonder the man got fat, looking huge in those glitter jumpsuits before he died. It was good stuff. He would make them all the time in his dorm room back in the day. All the offensive linemen would come over and each of them would put away three or four at one sitting. He'd heard that it had become tradition, that the line would get together on Thursday or Friday nights and sit around, carrying on what he started.

The second he got up, Tiras said, "Where you going?" Lil' Man told him nowhere, it's just that he felt like eating and asked Tiras if he wanted some. Tiras said, "What's wrong with you, nigga? I'm fucking stressin' over here and you hungry. You fucking fat enough already. You don't need to be eating no more of them goddamn sandwiches."

So much for that.

Kwame had gone to the back shed to check on them two boys they had beaten up the night before; past the crates of TEC-9s to a small room, no windows, one light bulb hanging from the center of the ceiling. He opened the door, checked to see that they were where they were left and closed the door without saying anything. He was pretty sure he could kill them right now and nobody would know the difference. Put a bullet in each of their heads. Like he wanted to do last night. But, no, Tiras didn't want that. Kwame could see his point: he didn't want to start having to worry about getting rid of bodies a couple days shy of a big deal.

Getting rid of them wouldn't be the problem. Staying rid of them was. It made him think of the time—one of Tiras's first big deals—right before he was going to sell two hundred grams of cocaine to a bunch of Peruvians, guys who were in a test run for one of the Cuban cartels. The night before, some nigga used to be with Tiras in the John Does mouthed off to him about some chick—something like he was hitting that pussy every night while Tiras was with her. Tiras didn't like that and he was going on about what he was going to do to that motherfucker, a lot like Kwame could hear him doing inside right now. Kwame went right up to Tiras and said, "I'll do it," not really sure if Tiras was even serious. Trying to make a name for himself at that time. He shot the guy in the balls first, like Tiras said to. Blew 'em right off. Then dumped the body off MacArthur Causeway in the middle of the night. It was a stupid move, looking back on it. Headlights kept coming in the distance, neon of the Miami skyline in the background. He had to stop what he was doing, twice, before he could get the job done. Drive back and forth, doubling back between Miami Beach and the mainland, before he saw there was no one coming in his direction. Lumped the body over his shoulder and walked it down to the seawall—not believing that no one saw his car sitting there on the side of the road, even at one o'clock in the morning. *Especially* because it was one o'clock in the morning. Must've not, though, because the body washed up in Government Cut, and they never got so much as a phone call. Tiras didn't care about that, though. Kwame remembered him saying, "What the fuck you doing?" In a calm voice scarier than when he would go off. He asked Kwame why he didn't take him out to the swamp, bury him in some mud. Uh-uh. Shoot, you don't know what's in there. Have some crocodile or gator or whatever the hell they had out there come up and take you in, do that death roll. Either that or them chiggers bite you, you come back with who-knows-what disease.

Still, Tiras told him, "You get your mind right."

He ain't fucked up since.

Kwame came back inside to the sound of Tiras's voice filling up the house. Sounding the same as when he went outside. Wasn't nothing he did. Wasn't his fault that white bread up and ran off. So he wasn't listening to none of that; that's what Lil' Man was here for. Kwame had more time in, so it was Lil' Man's turn to listen to that bitching. Lil' Man didn't even come back until he blew his knee and left The U. Else he might not have come back at all. Be off in the pros. Nope, just kick back, enjoy the high and wait to make some big money when that dude from Atlanta make it down here.

Before he could kick back, though, Kwame pushed the curtain aside on the front window, hearing a car door slam outside. "Awww, shit," he said. "We got company."

Murray saw the curtain move as he walked towards the house. He looked back to Nicky to make sure he wasn't making any nervous moves that might get them shot on the front lawn. He heard loud voices from inside the house, then heard them dissipate as he stopped on the front porch. The door opened before he had a chance to knock on it. Standing before him was Tiras, Lil' Man and another black guy behind them. Tiras said, "What you doing here?"

Murray looked over the three of them then back to Tiras when he said, "I was wondering if we could talk?"

"Talk?" Tiras said. "What the fuck we got to talk about?" Tiras moved his gaze to Nicky Silva. "Who this? Your new boyfriend?"

The one behind Tiras and Lil' Man grinned at them and said, "Yeah, that your new boyfriend? Y'all sucking each other's dicks?"

Murray ignored him and said, "Can we come in?"

Tiras smirked and moved away from the door. He sat down in the kitchen and said, "So, what we got to talk about?"

Murray put his hands on the back of the chair closest to the front door. "A lot of things. First, there was a car, a '57 Buick Century parked in the alley next to my building . . ."

"I don't know nothing about that."

"About what? About the guy who was driving it?"

"Hey, padnuh, you send two guys to my house in the middle of the night, it's gonna be them or me. And, it ain't gonna be me."

"Those guys were returning some people you sent to *my* house."

"I get what you saying, that you were just returning the favor. That you wasn't doing nothing that wasn't done to you first. I know all about that shit, boy. I been persecuted my whole life, and I fight back."

Murray said, "I don't know anything about your persecution. I do know that I asked a friend of mine to return something that I found on my doorstep, namely your goons."

"My 'goons?' " Tiras laughed and turned towards Lil' Man and the other one. "You going to come up in here and call my friends 'goons'? How you know it ain't these two?"

Murray said, pointing to Lil' Man, "I recognize him," and turned to the other one, "and I'm sure he wasn't one of them."

"That's Kwame. You might recognize him, though. He been to your house."

The three of them laughed.

Murray let it go.

Tiras said, "Since everybody seem to be in the introducing mood, who this?" turning his head towards Nicky Silva.

Murray said, "This is Nick. He's an associate."

"Nick. You an associate of Jack Murray here, huh?" Tiras said, smiling. "Fucking uptown, man."

Before he let Tiras go further, Murray said, "I'm glad everybody knows everybody now, but I have another question. Where's the guy that drove the car?"

"What car?"

"The Buick that showed up here last night."

"He around."

"What does that mean?"

"That mean he around. He alive, you don't have to worry yourself about that. If he was dead, I would've stuffed him in that car when I returned it to you. But, he ain't going nowhere just yet."

Murray took that to mean that he was close, maybe even inside the house. He nodded and said, "Why isn't he going anywhere just yet?"

"I got my reasons," Tiras said. "Next?"

"What about Rudy?"

"What about him? I went to his house this morning, he gone."

Murray said, "What're you talking about?"

"I just told you, man. I go by his house after I'm done dropping that car off and ain't nobody there. He supposed to be here so I can keep an eye on him. I go over there, his old lady ain't there, ain't no lights on. Not even the TV. And you know his old lady always in front of the TV, don't matter what time of day."

"He pussy anyway," Kwame said. "We don't need him for this shit."

Murray said, "Need him for what?"

Tiras gave Kwame a look and said, "That's some other business. You got that?" He turned to Murray. "That ain't nothing you need to worry about."

"What? You mean about the fact that you took part of the money I earned on a job with Rudy, bought some TEC-9s with it and are looking to make a bundle off one of Rudy's old partners? The guy named, I believe, Lloyd Bone."

There it was.

It didn't go over as bad as Murray thought it would. Not one of them said a thing. Lil' Man and the other one, Kwame, were just staring at him. Shit, Tiras was smiling. He said, "I guess you talked to Rudy."

"The night you broke into my building. You have to be quiet if you want to catch somebody off guard."

"How I know you ain't got him at your apartment right now, keeping him there for some insurance, trying to get in on my deal? How I know you didn't talk to him right before you came over here?"

"That's a fair question. You don't know. I imagine you'd be tempted to find out. You sure know the way to my house."

Tiras said, "If he ain't there, that's the end of your insurance policy."

"That doesn't mean he isn't somewhere else. Somewhere that Lloyd knows to contact him at."

"So what you after?"

"The way I see it, you need me. You need me because Lloyd Bone knows Rudy, he doesn't know you."

"Bullshit. Once I talk to the man brother to brother, ain't going to be no need for Rudy. I don't care how long they been knowing each other."

"Look, I don't know Lloyd personally. But, I do know he took Rudy under his wing a long time back now, practically right after he stopped sucking his momma's tit. So, you can try to talk to him. Y'all can touch fists and do all that shit. At the end of it, if he thinks he can trust you, you *might* get your money. You let me know how that goes."

Tiras glanced at Nicky Silva, then back to Murray. "What you want?"

"I want to be left alone. I want half of whatever you're getting from this deal, provided you get anything. You cut up your half any way you want."

"We can talk about it," Tiras said.

"We just did. You'll hear from me."

Murray walked out and Nicky Silva followed him out to the car, getting out of there without turning to look back.

"That went well," Murray said.

"I thought so," Nicky said. "You worked that room pretty good."

Yeah, that part even surprised Murray.

"But, who's this Rudy I keep hearing about?"

Miranda pulled up on Northwest Twenty-fourth to see a black Nissan Maxima parked outside Tiras's house. A-ha, so she would have something to report to Harvey if she ended up having to go to dinner with him tonight. She would let her agents take over for her then, preferring to get the ball rolling herself. She took out her notepad, having just enough of an angle to get the tag number on the Maxima. She had always taken good notes, one of the first things taught at the Academy and stressed to her by Bill Cecil when she came onboard.

She sat there, notepad in hand, and waited for something to happen. She started to write when she saw two guys come out and get in the car then stopped, her stomach turning over a bit. She remembered what Bill Cecil told her. Get it right, he said. Use the right words, keep it simple. Note the exact times somebody does something.

Okay.

Twelve-fifty-one P.M.

Jack Murray and unknown white male seen leaving Tiras Williams's house.

What Murray couldn't understand, if the deal was solid and Tiras didn't need Rudy to help close it with Lloyd, then why take on a partner? He had gone into Tiras's house and told him that he was in, point blank, and Tiras didn't even put up a fight. Nicky had said he thought it was because Murray had said he might have Rudy somewhere, that having Rudy around was good just that Tiras didn't want to admit it. Or, that maybe Tiras could pass Murray off as another of Rudy's partners, that it was better than nothing.

Murray considered another option—that Tiras was just telling him what he wanted to hear to shut him up—and thought about it all the way home and was still thinking about it when there was a knock on his door. He asked who it was through the door and heard a voice say, "Front desk." He opened up and a pear-shaped woman maybe in her early eighties, somebody's grandma, leaning on a derby walking cane, said, "Can you come down and check your messages every so often? It's hard for me to get up here."

Murray said, "Yes, ma'am," and watched her feel her way down the hall, the rubber stopper on her cane moving one step at a time, one hand against the wall, steadying her. He put the message in his pocket and helped her navigate the stairs. Downstairs, after getting her behind the reception desk, Murray took the yellow scrap paper out and looked at it.

It was the address for Miranda's apartment with the word "Gables" written underneath. And her home phone number in case he got lost.

The house in Bal Harbour where Nicky Silva was staying, one of the first waterfront lots on the Middle River, was the last house Caesar Pelli ever bought with his wife of fifty years. Caesar let Gina stay in it after his dear Gertrude passed. Now, she was waiting for the homeowner's association to come around asking where the annual association fee was; waiting for the utility company to call about Caesar's bill, which she sure as hell didn't have money to pay; then waiting for the lights to go out and the phone to be cut off. The feds had come by after Caesar's arrest. She had found out about that from one of Caesar's neighbors who watched the whole thing from her kitchen window. She didn't say they were with the FBI, but Gina could assume by the description. She was lucky she was somewhere else, out getting her hair and nails done, or else she'd be in custody. The next time, and she was sure there would be a next time, they would probably just come in and start confiscating things. Maybe she could get Nicky to move her vanity out of the upstairs bedroom.

Two o'clock, Gina heard Nicky Silva come back from his meeting with Jack Murray. She came into the entrance hall to catch Nicky flipping through the mail, not sure why he was doing that because none of it was his. She brought a towel up to her chest and said, "How'd it go?" Sounding like a wife.

Nicky said, "Okay."

She said, "Okay, that's it? I hope it was a lot better than just 'okay.' One of the neighbors told me there were some guys in suits, official looking, come by. She didn't say what they were, but you can probably guess."

Nicky said, "When?"

"Earlier today."

"They came inside?"

"She said they knocked and waited then left. They didn't leave anything."

"They won't leave anything next time either. Not even the furniture," Nicky said. "Where were you?"

"Out."

Christ. They didn't leave anything because they're going to come back, maybe today, start taking shit left and right, seizing property. They couldn't go to the boat. That would be the first thing they were going to auction off.

Gina said to Nicky, "What do you wanna do?"

"We'll need to leave 'cause they'll be back at some point," Nicky said. "But, I'm not going anywhere far until I get my money first."

Chapter Sixteen

The minute Miranda opened the door and said, "Hi," no expression on her face, Murray regretted coming over.

Maybe it was something he didn't know about, something that had nothing to do with him. He said, "Are you okay?"

She said, "Yes . . ." not sounding too sure about it. "Well, yes and no."

He looked closer at her, at her eyes, turning a pinkish red now from crying. "What's going on?"

"Nothing." But, then she closed the door behind him and said, "I wanted to talk to you."

He had heard that from her before and each time it was something that made him queasy. He was sure this was another surprise. They sat on the couch, and Miranda said, "I saw you coming out of Tiras Williams's house today."

Surprise.

That was it. No explaining what she was doing there, getting right to it. "I saw you coming out of Tiras Williams's house today." Boom. Like they were married and she saw him with a woman she might work with. It pissed him off, thinking this was some game she was playing with him. They were together last night. Then, she leaves, no note. Now, she's, what, spying on him?

She watched him and smiled. "I'll make some coffee."

Just like that, leaving him hanging. Casual about it.

Miranda was in the kitchen for a few minutes then came

back out again, saying, "Jack, I'm really sorry about last night. I'm not usually like that, I mean, just leaving. I'm not that type, and I know you were hurt."

That was something he could use. Instead, he said, "Don't worry about it. I'm sure something had come up. As long as you were okay."

She said, "I was," pouring their coffee.

Murray watched her lay the cups on coasters and sit down across from him, wondering if she was going to expand on her answer. When she didn't, he said, "What happened last night?" and felt justified in doing it.

"I got a call."

Murray wanted to ask from who. Maybe another man. She was a good-looking woman. He waited, taking sips to stretch it out. Finally, she said, "Actually, I went over to Rudy's."

And he stopped sipping, half-choking on the coffee going down.

"When you say you went to Rudy's . . ."

She gave him a look and said, "Not like *that*. The call was from Faye. I had been over there once and left her my card, hoping she'd call me in case he ever came back around."

"How'd you know about Faye?"

"You went there after we left Fairchild Garden. I followed you."

"You followed me?"

So she was spying on him . . .

"I'm interested in you," Miranda said, "okay?"

. . . but it was alright.

"I had a good idea of what kind of guy you were, but I wasn't sure. And I wanted to be sure. I did my homework."

"You sure have the resources." Murray took another sip, trying to think if there was ever another woman who had done that before. "That's thorough."

Miranda stared at him over her coffee mug and said, "You want some more?"

Murray shook his head and brought his mug down to the coffee table. He said, "Are you the reason Rudy and Faye are gone?"

"How do you know they're gone? Is that what you were doing over at Tiras's house, talking about Rudy?"

"That was part of it. Me and him, we had some things to straighten out."

"What kind of things?"

He said, "Things."

She noticed he was smiling, just a little. Like he didn't want to say anymore. She smiled back and said, "Are these the kinds of things I should be worried about?"

Murray said, "No," and meant it. Honestly, he couldn't see why anything he had to do with Tiras could be of professional interest to her; she was busy wrapping up her part of Caesar's arrest.

"Because now I'm investigating Tiras."

"What do you mean you're 'investigating' Tiras?"

"I mean I'm hoping to head a federal investigation into Tiras Williams and his organization."

Okay, maybe she would have some interest.

"I'm not sure he has what you would call an 'organization,' but that certainly is interesting." Murray thought about how he could use that information, seeing his current situation.

"That's what I was doing when I saw you. I was getting it started. Then I came home."

"And that's it for today?"

"No, I have two agents working for me."

"They're at his house right now?"

Miranda nodded.

Murray told himself to remember that, something else he could use.

"When I saw you," Miranda said, "I came home because I wasn't feeling so good all of a sudden. I called in sick for the rest of the day, mostly so I could get out of going to dinner with my boss."

"What, your boss asked you out to dinner? You two do that often?"

"Never. It was kind of unexpected."

"He your type?"

"Not at all. He's a little mouse of a guy. The collars on his shirts are too big for his neck."

Murray was quiet, content to watch the expression on Miranda's face while she described how narrow her boss's head was. Enjoying watching her. When he thought she was finished, he said, "Miranda, I have to be honest with you."

"About what?"

"Tiras has a deal coming up that I'm trying to get in on."

Miranda stared at her hand resting on the top of her knee, legs curled against her under a loose t-shirt. She concentrated on the tip of her index finger and said, "Were you going to tell me about this?"

"That's what I'm doing."

"You want to tell me more?"

"He's looking to arrange for the sale of TEC-9s," Murray said. "He's got a buyer lined up, a guy that Rudy used to do business with named Lloyd Bone, from Atlanta. The only problem, Rudy's not around anymore. I'm not entirely sure Rudy is a necessity for the deal to go through, but I think the buyer was at least expecting to have him around, considering he's the one that introduced them."

"I gave him and Faye some money, whatever I had on me, to leave."

"You don't know where they went?"

"I didn't want to know. He was in so far over his head, I felt bad for both of them. Faye may still have my card, but who knows?"

"That might make things difficult."

Miranda said, "Jack, why would you tell me this?"

"I was thinking maybe I could work for you."

"What do you mean 'work for' me?"

"I could give you information."

"You want to work undercover for me?"

"Why not? You could probably use it, couldn't you? You were doing it, right? And I have a lot more experience dealing with these types of guys than you do, all due respect to your academy training."

"I don't know. It'll be really dangerous."

"Look, these guys are dangerous. But, I'm already in deep with them. That's actually the beauty of it. I'm not going to shake this guy by myself, I've already tried. And this could be good for you. Besides, they're not very smart. I'm not going to wear a wire, but, short of that, I don't think they'd catch on."

"I was thinking more about my boss. If I used you as an informant, you'd be opening yourself up to all sorts of scrutiny."

"I thought you said he was a little mouse."

"That's as a person. As a boss, he can be a real asshole." She let it roll around in her head a little bit, weighing the possibilities. "I'm not sure about it."

"What's not to be sure about? If I'm in trouble, you'll be close by, right?"

She nodded her head. "I'll consider it."

Murray took her cup and lowered it to the coffee table.

"While you're doing that," he said, "what're we going to do in the meantime?"

★ ★ ★ ★ ★

Later, Miranda's head nestled on his chest as the orange haze from fading sun came through her window, the Alhambra Water Tower visible in the distance. Murray lay there, eyes wide open, thinking about what was coming next. He liked the idea that they were working on this together, some secret operation. Like some private eye couple in the old TV shows. Like *McMillan and Wife*. He would be the Rock Hudson character, only straight, and she would be the Susan Saint James character, only smart. And, they wouldn't be married. And, Murray wasn't sure that they were actually private eyes. Rock Hudson might have worked for the city. Maybe there was another show he could think of.

He liked the idea of getting Tiras Williams out of his life. He wasn't lying when he told Miranda he couldn't do that by himself. How would he? She had already busted anybody that could help him. He knew that wasn't her fault, though.

Most of all, she had given him some information that he could use; this time, he liked the idea of giving her something she could use.

Him.

Murray didn't see Lil' Man until he was almost to his front door. There he was, standing in the crook at the end of the hall. It was seven P.M. now. How long had he been there? Murray said, "What are you doing here?" and wondered how many people had asked him the same question.

Lil' Man said, "You didn't think you were gonna get off that easy did you?" not answering the question.

"What is this? Another try? Like I told your boss, you have to surprise people, catch them off guard, for that to work. Not stand in the hallway, waiting for me to come home. It would've worked better if you were *inside* my apartment."

Lil' Man thought about telling Murray he could put one in his head right here in the hall. *Outside.* See how smart he was then.

They stared at each other for a minute, each of them looking like they were expecting the other one to say something. Until Murray got tired of it and unlocked the door.

Lil' Man put his hand on the door as Murray was closing it and followed him in. Murray gave him a look like, What the fuck are you doing? and Lil' Man said, "I need you to let me see Rudy."

"You serious?"

Lil' Man kept staring, not saying anything.

Murray said, "Tiras sent you over here to make sure I have him?"

"He say not to leave until I seen him."

"Well," Murray said, "he's not here. I know enough to not keep him in a place you know about. There's no fucking way I'm calling him, either, so you can forget about that."

Murray sat on his sofa, not minding what Lil' Man was doing. Fuck him. Let him stand there all night if he wants to. He said, "We can watch TV if you want to. It's gonna be a long wait."

Lil' Man said, "No, it ain't." Jack saw Lil' Man reach down towards his waistband. Saw it out of the corner of his eye, Murray trying to give the impression that he wasn't looking at Lil' Man, aware of any move he might make. Murray moved to his right and his hand went under a throw pillow, coming out with the .22 he had gotten into the habit of keeping under there.

He watched the look on Lil' Man's face, surprise, and said, "Another thing that you'll learn is not to keep your gun way down in your pants like that. Makes it harder to get the drop on somebody, especially when you have to get around all that belly of yours. What I want you to do is undo your jeans, slowly and with your left hand, and let them drop to the floor."

"What are you, some kinda freak?"

"It's to get your gun away from your hands," Murray said. "You got the safety on?"

Lil' Man shook his head.

"Then do it carefully."

Lil' Man undid the button and zipper, having a little trouble with it, and let his jeans down around his ankles. He kicked them loose like Murray told him to.

"Now," Murray said, "go over there and get a chair from the table and pull it over here." Murray picked up the jeans and pistol, some kind of automatic he didn't recognize, while Lil' Man did that. He sat back down and looked at Lil' Man, feeling sorry for this man, this kid, sitting across from him in his t-shirt and underwear.

Lil' Man said, "What're we gonna do now?"

"Now you're going to tell me a little about yourself. First, your name."

Lil' Man looked away, unimpressed, and waved a hand at Murray.

"We can do that or you can walk out of here like you are, and I don't mean walking back to your car. The keys are in the pocket of your jeans, right? Then, we can tell Tiras you saw me but couldn't get the job done. Whereas you cooperate, maybe you can say I never showed up."

Lil' Man sighed and said, "My name's Marion."

"That's your name, huh? No wonder you want to go by a nickname."

"My mom's from PG County, M*urr*yland. She liked Marion Barry, named me after him."

"Marion what?"

"Williams, man," Lil' Man said. "What the fuck you need to know all this for?"

"I like to know who I'm doing business with, Marion." Not saying anything more than that. "Where are you from?"

"Kendall."

"That's a decent neighborhood. They got some good working-class people there. What are you doing hanging around with a guy like Tiras for?"

Lil' Man shrugged, but had a look in his eye like maybe he was thinking about it.

"Before that," he said, "I was on football scholarship to Miami. 'Til I blew out my knee. Spent over a year in rehab, but lost my eligibility." Then, with a sound of interest in his voice, "I was on the Dolphin practice squad for a couple years, though."

"No shit?" Murray said. "What position?"

When they got back to the motel, Rudy gave Faye some money and told her to go next door, to the store, and get some cigarettes. She looked at the money and said, "That's it? Can I get a little bit more so I can get a candy bar or something?" Rudy told her, shit, they just ate, wasn't that enough? She said, "I'd *like* a candy bar, please," and got two more dollar bills.

But it was starting to rain. And, she didn't want to go out in the rain, get her hair all wet. Faye gave the bills back to Rudy and told him to go on, get her a pack of the cheapest brand they had, long as they were menthol, and a bag of chocolate-covered raisins. That way she could pretend like she was at the movies watching whatever was on HBO and eating chocolate-covered raisins, like they had in the concession stand at the picture show. But, the channel that was supposed to be HBO wasn't. She didn't know what it was, but it looked like PBS or something, some program about politics on. The sign in front of the motel said "Free HBO." That's why they stopped.

She flipped though other channels, but they were all local

and, at this time of night, all that was on was the news.

When Rudy came back in, protecting her cigarettes and chocolate covered raisins from the rain, Faye said, "We got to go back home. They ain't got shit for TV shows here."

Miranda told Bill Cecil, "I was having trouble sleeping."

He said, "Really?" leaning over to look at the clock that read 10:24. "The missus went up earlier to read. I guess I fell asleep waiting for *Sportscenter*."

She told him about her investigation that she started that afternoon. "I went to Tiras's house, out on Northwest Twenty-fourth." She heard Bill tell her about being careful, a young woman out there by herself. She told him it was alright, she could take care of herself. Then, said, "The two guys you got for me took over after that."

"That was pretty quick. When we talked before you sounded like you were going to do the whole thing by yourself."

"Yeah, well, I wasn't feeling too good."

"Maybe that's why you can't sleep."

"No, that was something else."

Miranda had a problem telling other people they were right. She found it hard to do being a woman in law enforcement. They already saw a female as a secretary more than anything. She didn't see the usefulness in giving them more reason to do that. But, if there was someone she didn't mind admitting it to . . .

"You were right about Jack Murray," she said.

"He was there?"

"I pulled up, and he walked out about ten minutes later."

"What'd you do?"

"Like I said, I came home."

"That was it?"

"Then I invited him over."

"Is he still there?"

"We wouldn't be talking if he was," she said. "He left a little while ago."

"Oh, dear."

"It was okay. He admitted to me that he was involved in a deal with Tiras, but that he really wasn't into it. He says Tiras is trying to sell a stock of TEC-9s to a buyer that's coming down from Atlanta. I told him that I'm launching a criminal investigation of Tiras."

"This sounds like it'll work out fine."

"Don't be so cynical. He ended up asking to work undercover for me."

"You should watch out. You could get into trouble with that," Bill Cecil said. "Well, that's certainly a way for the two of you to bond."

"I thought so. I mean, he made some good points. He has a lot of experience dealing with guys like this. And he wants to get rid of Tiras Williams as bad as I do."

"Is he serious?"

"Yeah," she said. "He said he's not going to wear a wire, but, besides that, he could pass me all the information I need."

"You trust him?"

"Yeah." She took a moment. "We have a unique relationship. Sure, there's some self-interest there. Basically, to untangle himself from a situation he's gotten into. That kind of disclosure actually makes me trust him more. When he first offered, I knew this was part of the reason and he admitted it."

"If you do this . . . well, have you figured out how you're going to do this? I mean, how much are you going to let Harvey in on? Eventually, he'll have to know."

"I'm working on that," she said. "*That's* why I couldn't sleep."

"When's their next meeting?"

"He's not sure yet. Let me ask you this. Can this deal go off if the middleman's not around? The guy who introduced Tiras to his buyer has disappeared."

"If Tiras doesn't know the guy, yeah, that could make it tricky. There has to be a certain level of trust or security or whatever word you want to use. Some of that is lost if the contact is not there. You don't know where that guy is?"

"I gave him and his girlfriend some money to leave town."

"Why?"

"Because I felt sorry for them."

"You know, you can sidestep all this if Murray knows where the guns are."

"He didn't say anything about that."

"If he did, you could pick Tiras up tonight for possession of illegal weapons or unregistered firearms or selling without a license. If you get to him after the deal's done, you only get the money. That won't do you any good."

Miranda said, "I know," and paused. "What would you do?"

"I'd try to find out about the guns before any of this ever goes down. That way you get your man and, hopefully, keep your boyfriend."

"I told you he's not after the money. He wants to get this guy out of his way."

"Yeah, but for what? I mean, what's he planning to do after that? You think that the two of you are going to walk hand in hand on the beach? If all that money starts changing hands . . . that does funny things to people. You get the guns early, you take that uncertainty out of play."

"So you're not convinced he's being honest with me?"

"Not yet. I don't know his life history, but he is where he is for a reason. A demonstrated absence of normalcy. He hasn't done anything with his life, and, all of a sudden, he wants to do the right thing?"

"You sound optimistic."

"I just don't want to have to say I told you so."

It was almost eleven, and Tiras still hadn't heard from Lil' Man. Been calling him on his cell, leaving messages on his answering machine; even called his momma's house. Had to look the number up in the phone book. Nothing. Finally, saw the headlights and heard the engine of his own Escalade, a big monster roar of 400-plus horsepower, pull into the driveway.

He stood at the window, looking, came outside and said, "Where you been?"

The sound of the door slamming then, "I been waiting like you told me."

"You ain't got your phone on you?"

"I got it," Lil' Man said, walking past Tiras up the front steps.

Inside, Tiras said, "I been calling you."

"I turned it off. I'm waiting around in the dark, waiting to surprise the man and my phone goes off. What you want?"

"You leave it on vibrate then."

Lil' Man shrugged it off and got pissed when Tiras said, "I even called your momma's house."

"Don't do that."

Taking offense, Lil' Man squared off on Tiras. Tiras, feeling hot breath on his face, had decided earlier that he was going to stay calm for Lil' Man's benefit. Over three hours trying to get ahold of him.

Tiras said, "He never show up?"

Lil' Man shook his head. "I came straight here from there."

Tiras sat down saying, "Yeah, well, I know he ain't gonna do nothing without my say-so. I got the merchandise even if he got that punk-ass Rudy. And, the merchandise is what everybody wants. So what I got to say to Jack Murray is buuullls*hit*. Way I see it, I got a couple of moves I can make here."

"Like what?"

"First, I give that cracker one last chance to tell me where Rudy is. He come in here frontin' on me like it's his deal. Shit. Second, he wants to play big shot, I'm gonna let him. He can represent if he want to."

"What you talking about?"

"I'm gonna let him be a big part of this deal. He going to be my representative. He going to walk up to Mister Lloyd Bone and say, 'How you doing Mister Bone? Can I interest you in a few dozen guns today?' "

"You going to let him do that?"

"Why not? He got Rudy and Rudy so all-fire important, right? They can do it together. Then, Mister Jack Murray gonna get greedy. You see, he want the guns *and* the money all for hisself. He going to shoot Rudy and try to shoot Lloyd Bone, a friend of his come down from Atlanta. Only thing, Mister Bone too fast for Jack. Shot him trying to defend himself."

"What about Lloyd Bone? He ain't going to watch you pop up and shoot two people and then want to go on talking to you. That's crazy talk."

"I think about that one. I imagine if things get out of line, Lloyd Bone might get shot too. Maybe Jack Murray gets off a miracle shot. Laying on the ground, bleeding, he gets Lloyd right in the chest. Like they do in the movies."

"What about everything we been doing? We still gonna have these guns."

"Yeah, but we got the money too," Tiras said. "As for the guns, I'll unload them, no problem."

"Why not start looking for somebody else right now then? Why even go through all that trouble?"

" 'Cause my reputation been damaged and Jack Murray done it. He been playin' me, making me look like a fool. I don't want it getting around that Tiras Williams is a fool. I'm doing this for personal pride. That something you should've learned in football 'fore you dropped out."

Lil' Man let that one go and said, "You know Lloyd's not coming alone. That ain't ever going to work if he has his people with him."

"That's a good point," Tiras said. "Ah, maybe they hear some shots. From, say, behind a building close by. They get nervous and start shooting in Jack Murray's direction. They probably get off a few rounds, bound to hit something. On their way out, they get ambushed and get their money stolen."

"You still got Jack and Rudy."

"At that point, they don't trust nobody. Not even each other. They start shooting it out, end up killing one another."

Tiras paused.

"Thanks, padnuh," he said. "I think I like that plan better."

When Kwame came back inside, not paying attention to Tiras and Lil' Man in the living room, he went for the kitchen. Straight for the stovetop burner to cook up some meth and chill for a while.

Tiras came in after him and said, "You take some, but watch that stuff for the rest of the night. Lil' Man said Jack Murray never come home this evening."

Kwame nodded and said, "You want me to hold off? What, you want some? We got plenty."

Tiras shook his head. "I need you sharp for tomorrow morning. He got to go home sometime." The wait for the burner made Tiras change his mind, and he snuck a hit before Kwame. He felt it run through him, thinking about his master plan.

He said, "This time we gonna go."

The first thing Faye did after turning on the TV was go to the refrigerator and check the milk. It had gone bad, and she dry heaved a few times pouring it down the sink. Clumps coming out at times. After that, she grabbed a can of soda and relaxed on the couch. She lit a cigarette and pulled an ashtray close to her, a clean one, new from the motel they just left. There was something else she had to do but couldn't remember.

She reached back for her robe draped over the back of the couch and felt for the shape of that lady agent's card inside the pocket.

Oh, yeah, call her up, ask if there was anything else she could do for them. Maybe ask her for some more money. Enough for a *ho*tel this time, one with good TV channels.

Chapter Seventeen

Murray dialed the number Miranda had given him, the office phone on her business card. He was wondering if that's what they were now, business, when he heard a voice on the other end saying, "You've reached . . ." and started to speak to it before he realized it was her voice mail. He was silent as the message went on, then hung up. She had told him to call this morning, see if she had made up her mind about his offer. He had a good feeling about it overnight, waking up excited about what he might be doing. Now that feeling nose-dived a bit.

He tried to put it out of his mind while he made his bed for the first time, not counting prison time, since he was a kid. Maybe seven or eight. That would make it somewhere between twenty-four or twenty-five years since he'd made his own bed as a civilian. Whew. His dad was never too strict about that sort of thing, keeping his room neat or picking up after himself. He was too busy busting his ass. His mom wasn't either, but for different reasons. Soon enough, her alcohol intake stopped her from caring about just about anything. Which is why his dad dumped her, sent her back to her mother in Trenton, telling her that if she couldn't mind Jack while he was out earning, he would find someone who could or do it himself.

Now, Murray had made his bed when he knew when Miranda was coming over and occasionally when he knew ahead of time that he was going to have a lady friend over. But, it wasn't first thing in the morning like regular people do, so he wasn't sure if that counted. He was finishing up, tucking the end of the blanket under the pillow when he noticed something behind him moving in front of the light coming through windows in the living area. Good thing he made the bed, maybe she came over to get him. It would make a good impression. He turned and looked over his shoulder.

"What you doing?" Tiras said, Kwame standing in back of him.

Fucking shit, he'd have to remember to do a better job of locking his door.

"Straightening up," a mixture of disappointment and something else, maybe worry, in Murray's voice.

"When you finish playing house, we need to talk."

Whatever it was, Murray hoped it wouldn't take too long.

Faye had the chain on the door, and when she saw Miranda through the narrow opening, she said, "Oh," and lowered her eyes while undoing the chain. The door closed all the way, then opened, and she said, "You got my message?"

"I did," Miranda said. "Can I come in?"

Miranda sat down, looking around to see that not much had changed since she was here last. Two days ago. She sat up on the couch, not wanting to sit back against the pillows, cigarette smoke and mildew smell seeped into it. She said, "You weren't gone very long."

"We went up Dixie Highway over to Punta Gorda," Faye said. "We wasn't going to have enough money to go far or for a long time. Rudy didn't have no big ideas on how to get any money, either. That's why we came back, why I called you."

Miranda waited while Faye lighted a cigarette.

"You want more money?"

"It would help," Faye said. "I mean, we ain't got shit. And that little bit you gave us, all due respect, didn't go that far."

"I'm not really sure I can do that."

"How about the people you work for? Maybe they could give us something if Rudy helps them out."

It was a thought. Miranda knew there was no way that it could happen; no way that her boss would approve paying an informant for aiding an investigation. They might get something.

But probably not what they were looking for.

"Where is Rudy now?" Miranda said.

"He's upstairs sleeping. He been sleeping since we got back."

"I thought you said you didn't want Rudy to get involved."

Faye stared at her. "I recall that I said I didn't want Rudy to get hurt." She paused to smoke. "Them's two different things, getting involved and getting hurt."

Nine-thirty in the morning, Special Agents Ken Phelps and Michael Taylor had Tiras Williams's house under surveillance. Getting bored with it now, having been on a little over a full day but doing the same thing for Miranda before that, only at a different address.

They watched the house, a white wood frame bungalow, from far enough down Twenty-fourth Avenue where they couldn't be seen but still with a view. They waited, wondering when Tiras was going to come back, his having left about a half hour ago.

"What do you think is going on in there?" Taylor said what they were both thinking.

Phelps shrugged. "I could speculate for you. It'd be guns or drugs. Maybe there's something more."

"Maybe some terrorist activity?" Excitement in Taylor's voice. "You think he could be hiding bomb-making materials in there?"

"I'm not sure about that," Phelps said. "I think they'd have wanted to bust his front door down by now if that was the case." He stopped and thought about it. "I wish she would tell us more."

"What do you think about her?"

"She's fucking sexy," Phelps said. "She looks good in a suit. Looks good in skirts, too. Articulate but with a hint of a Spanish accent. I like that type. Nice hair, too."

"I know," Taylor said. "I wouldn't mind getting with her either. The thing I like about her . . ."

Taylor stopped talking. A car, a white El Dorado, turned onto Twenty-fourth Avenue off Northwest Eighty-fifth, pulled to a stop in front of Tiras's house, inched up, and then reversed into his driveway.

Taylor grabbed binoculars from the glove compartment and said, "Who do we have here?" He saw a young black male, five-nine, no more than twenty to twenty-five but looking older, carrying over two hundred pounds, walk up the front porch and look in a window. Saw him come back down to the drive and saw the passenger door open. A second black male, same age range, same height, probably in the neighborhood of one-fifty stepped from the car.

Phelps said, "What the fuck do you think this is?"

"I have no idea," Taylor said, looking hard through the binoculars. "I missed the tag number the first time they passed. Man, they could be doing anything."

They saw the car shake and the silhouette of the trunk open and close, wild privet over-growing on the chain link fence blocking a full view. They kept quiet watching three black males, the third one coming out of Tiras's house, standing between the El Dorado and the porch, talking. Their eyes would move up and down the street every so often until each of them pounded the other's fist and the El Dorado started out from the driveway.

"I want to take him," Phelps said. "This could be a key to the investigation."

"If we take him, then there would be no more investigation."

Taylor already had his phone out. "I'm gonna call this in."

Faye drew on her cigarette again.

She said to Miranda, "Like I also said, especially if you get that Tiras Williams. That man ain't fit to walk around in polite society."

"Maybe I should talk to Rudy about this."

"Don't worry about him." Faye stopped when Miranda checked her cell phone and started when she looked back up. "He going to do it if I tell him to."

At least she didn't need convincing.

Miranda said, "Those are details I'll have to discuss with Rudy," and excused herself. She wanted to step outside, check her message and come back in, planning to sit down with both of them. She could see how it would happen: Rudy wouldn't want to do it; Faye was all for it, which meant, eventually he would be all for it. They wouldn't get what they want, money, but they didn't have to know that right now. She would have to think of something.

As she started through her purse, Miranda saw Faye about to speak and saw her jump at a sound coming from the back of the house, somewhere. Maybe the back door rattling.

"You have a back door?" Miranda said.

Faye nodded, upright in her chair.

Miranda was already across the living room, kicking off her high heels on the way, when Faye pointed in a general direction like she was telling her, Yeah, it's back there somewhere.

She heard voices on the other side of the door, two of them, sounding like they were trying to make a decision on something. She got into position, her Beretta in two hands, parallel to the door, against the kitchen cabinetry, and looked over her shoulder. Faye was watching from the kitchen doorway, robe pulled close to her. Miranda waved her back, waving her gun for Faye to get out of there. But, it was too late to say anything to her, tell her where to go, as a plate of glass on the door window shattered. A hand came through, toggled the lock and the door came busting open. Two guys, they looked Hispanic to Miranda but they pushed in so fast she couldn't be sure, went by her followed by two others. Black men. One of them was going for one of the Hispanics, looking like he might try to kick him while he was down, while the other one glanced up at Faye in the kitchen doorway.

He said, "What we got here?" and moved towards Faye, halfway across the room before he stopped and turned.

Miranda had the front sight of her 9-millimeter in the middle of his chest. "I'm a special agent for the Federal Bureau of Investigation," she said, "and you're both under arrest."

The black man right in front of her turned halfway to smile at the other one and then took off down a hallway that ran through the middle of the house, all in one motion. Miranda cut him off by passing through the dining area, guessing he was going for the front door. As he reached for it, Miranda threw her body against his, the first thing she could think to do in that situation. He was bigger than she was, that was sure, but he was already stumbling when he reached for the door and her angle threw him off balance. She quickly pulled the asp baton out of the sheath on her waistband, flicked her wrist and the shaft extended out from the grip. She backed off, getting the room she needed to bring the steel across his shin and heard him yell, "Fuck!" She turned him face down on the floor and handcuffed his hands behind his back.

She turned when she heard Faye yelling out, calling for help. Miranda was certain she was going to have a hostage situation on her hands, wondering what weapon the other one had pressed up against Faye. She could tell by the echo of Faye's voice that they were near the hallway that ran down the middle of the house. Miranda circled back through the kitchen, her steps light, bare feet silent against the linoleum tile.

She peeked around the kitchen doorframe and saw the second black man holding Faye in front of him with what looked like a kitchen knife. Pressed against the side of her neck. Something he probably didn't bring along with him, not prepared for this type of thing. As he started to turn his body and Faye's, Miranda stepped forward and put the muzzle of her Beretta against his skull.

He stopped cold and held there for a moment before saying, "I could shove this knife in and she'd be dead."

"You'd be next," Miranda said.

He pressed the point of the knife against the flesh of Faye's neck.

Miranda said, "Do that again, you're dead."

"You ain't got the balls, bitch."

"I'd start with yours and work my way up from there. You're talking to an agent of the FBI, in case you missed that earlier. Your situation is hopeless. You want to go on?"

Miranda stared at the back of his head, pressing the muzzle tighter against his skin and saw his shoulders sag and saw his arms come down and heard the knife hit the floor. She kicked the man's feet out from under him, got him on his knees and took out a second pair of handcuffs from the snap case on her waistband.

She looked up and saw Faye massaging her neck, staring at the man face down in her kitchen. Then, she asked Faye to get her bag from the living room. On the way, she heard Faye open a bedroom door off the middle hall.

"How you like that?" Faye said, closing the door. "All that noise, Rudy didn't even wake up."

Miranda said, "You should wake him now," and dialed the mobile number she knew was for Agent Phelps or Taylor, she couldn't remember. Taylor picked up and she heard him saying that he was trying to call her, tell her about two unidentified black men leaving Tiras Williams's house.

The way Murray understood what Tiras told him was that if he wanted to earn his half, he would have to play a bigger role. "Going to have to step up," was how Tiras put it. Murray asked what he meant by that.

Tiras said, "You going to do this deal for me."

"What are you talking about?"

"You going to be my face in front of Lloyd Bone, make the exchange for me."

"Why would you want to do that? He doesn't even know me. He'll never go for that." Thinking he was making a good argument.

Tiras said, "I'll take care of that."

Murray said, "Where are you going to be?"

"I'm gonna be around."

Around. Sounding casual about it.

"What kind of shit is that? I'm going to get my cut because I practically delivered you the money to get this deal going in the first place. I'm the one who had to do the time while Rudy was on the outside."

Tiras said, "Well, that wouldn't have worked if you both would've gotten away. Speaking of Rudy, he going to be crucial to this 'cause he going to be front and center with you."

Murray thought about the gun he had under the throw pillow on his sofa. The one he had pulled on Lil' Man yesterday. Man, that thing was coming in handy. And would've been handy this time if Kwame wasn't sitting there. Right in the middle of the sofa. They caught Murray by surprise, making his bed, when they came in. By the time he talked them back into the living area, the first thing Kwame did was sit there. Making himself at home.

Murray believed he could walk around the coffee table, slowly, and get close to that end of the sofa before they might get suspicious, wondering what he was up to. Too much time would pass before he could get under the pillow, thinking they'd probably hold him down and look under there, find out what he was after. He was thinking about how to get to the .22, not that he could ask Kwame to get up, that wouldn't accomplish anything, when Tiras said to him, "So where Rudy at?"

Murray was still thinking about angles that he could take, about the possibilities should something happen when he said, "He's around," giving that attitude back.

"You getting quite the mouth on you, you know that?" Tiras said. "I know he around. I sent Lil' Man over here last night. He said you didn't come back, and he didn't see Rudy. I came over here this morning half-expecting to see him."

Murray started to say, "Like I told . . ." and stopped. "He's not here, where you'd know to come looking. I'm not calling him, either."

"When I sent Lil' Man over here, I told him not to leave without putting his eyes on Rudy. Suppose I tell you the same thing right now?"

"He's in a safe place."

"You hanging on to your insurance policy, huh?"

"Hey, if you trust me enough to send me out there to do your business for you, you should trust me about this. I want to get paid, too. It's in my best interest."

"I'm trying to understand what you're saying," Tiras said. "You ain't going to let me see Rudy and I'm supposed to trust that you going to show up with him when I tell you."

"That sounds about right."

"When you going to have him for me?"

"I'll talk to him this afternoon. After that, I'll call you, and we'll set it up."

"I'll be waiting for that phone call." Tiras ran his index finger over his upper lip, thinking about something, looking at Kwame over on the sofa. "You got to see this from my point of view. I got a lot riding on this. I can't just leave it up to chance."

"So do I," Murray said. "That's my point of view."

Chapter Eighteen

Miranda brought Murray in through the back way at the building on Northwest Second. Brought him to an office he figured wasn't hers, not enough stuff in it. Things on the desk, maybe a picture of her mom and dad, a diploma hanging on the wall, etc.; stuff he could see a woman having in her office.

Murray said, "This is where you work?" wondering what answer he would get.

"No, this is an empty office. A space that people use from time to time. When it's open."

Murray watched Miranda leaf through papers in a manila folder on the desk before he said, "Why don't we use your office?" Curious about what hers looked like.

"It's hectic down that way." She shut the folder and looked up at him. "I've had a busy morning."

Murray said he knew the feeling, not really sure if he did but just to keep the conversation going, then was silent while he waited for her to say something.

Miranda did say, "How was yours?" with an off-hand tone that told Murray she didn't think that it was important or that she was setting up to say something else.

"Tiras came by to see me, brought Kwame with him."

See if she was expecting that.

He watched her go upright in her chair. "What happened?"

"Nothing, really. He said he wants to see Rudy. I told him I'd talk to Rudy and get back to him. That'll hold him for a little while."

"I can help you with that," Miranda said. Not elaborating. "First, I want you to have this cell phone. You call me when something's going on, you find out new information, anything at all. Hit recall-one-send and it'll go straight to me."

Murray nodded and took the phone in the palm of his hand, the whole thing fitting with room to spare. "I never had one of these," he said, flipping it open to see the logo for the phone company and all the little buttons. Looking like the ones he'd see in the television commercials.

Miranda was watching him look at the phone, examining the thing, when she said, "Wait here a minute," and disappeared out into the hallway.

Murray waited, speculating on how long he would be waiting. Thinking maybe this secret government agent work wasn't as exciting as he thought it might be. He heard footsteps in the outer hallway getting closer, the hard bottom of a woman's high heels against the floor, then heard the door behind him open. He turned to see Miranda's head in the doorway.

"Jack, you want to come with me?"

Murray followed her down the hall, taking time to look around. Not at her backside, like he normally would, but at everything else. Professional-looking people in good suits going to work in a professional-looking place. Certainly a step up from any law enforcement building he'd been in. Well, that's the FBI for you, a step up.

Miranda took him down three different hallways—he counted them—past rows of closed office doors, a clump of cubicles in a common area. New people working their way toward an office, that was the same everywhere, in all walks. Finally, into a small room, narrow but about ten to twelve feet long, three windows along the wall to the left from where they entered.

"This is our interview area," Miranda said. "I want you to tell me if you recognize him."

She pointed to the window closest to them, and Murray stepped forward to the one-way glass, looking at a skinny black man, anxiety on his face, pulling up a metal chair to a metal table.

He said, "I think his name is Malik."

"Dade County has his name on file as Malik Merriweather Junior."

Murray nodded at hearing the full name, genuinely interested.

"He's got a long list of offenses," Miranda said. "How did you know him?"

"He was waiting for me at my building a couple of nights ago. I think Tiras sent him."

"For what?"

Murray shrugged, deciding she could figure out the rest.

Miranda said, "What happened?"

"Fortunately, I saw them before they saw me. I faked them out. I was lucky."

"You faked them out? What does that mean?"

Murray said, "That means I pulled a gun on them before they could get one on me," giving her his serious tone. "Then I got a friend to bring them back to Tiras's house."

He could see her making mental notes. She took him by the arm to the next window and said, "How about him?"

Murray recognized the face but had to think. "He was with Malik that night." He had it, Donny, but saw Miranda about to speak.

"Darnell Donald Joseph. You've never seen him before or after?"

Murray shrugged.

She took him to the third window. Chuco he recognized right away and somebody else. He said, "His name is Rafael Rojas," and pointed. "I don't know the other one."

She said, "How do you know Rafael?" not giving the second one's name.

"Me and Rafael did a weekend in lockup a long time ago. That was how we first met. We've been on odd jobs since. I see him now and then . . ."

"At social functions?"

She said that with a dry smile, and Murray started to lighten. He didn't let it show but felt a pressure start to lift, like they were back to talking like they used to.

"Not many of those in our life," he said, trying to keep the tone light, "but we'd go on jobs occasionally. You remember I told you I called a friend to take these other two back to Tiras's?" He waited while she nodded. "He's the friend."

"That's some friend," Miranda said. "How'd that happen?"

"I got them in the back of their car . . ."

"What kind of car is it?"

"I don't remember the make. But I called Rafael and I guess he needed a friend to drive his car, so they'd have a way to get home."

"You know what happened from there?"

Murray shook his head. "I found Rafael's car, a '57 Buick Century, in the alley outside my building the next day, so I figured something went wrong. They were just supposed to drop Malik's car and leave."

"Why didn't you drop the car?"

"I needed some time," he said, leaving out details. "How did you find all of these people?" Asking what he thought was the crucial question.

"We should talk back in the office."

Tiras got home, dropping off Kwame before going to the Popeye's off Seventh Avenue for a two-piece, dark meat, a side of red beans. All the lights off in the middle of the afternoon. Kwame, laid out on the recliner, didn't move when Tiras opened the door. Not even when he pushed it back open and let it slam. He didn't see Lil' Man, but he was around somewhere.

Tiras set the bag on the kitchen table and walked back into the living room, stepping heavy, the little wood house frame shaking on its piers. He tapped Kwame on the leg and said, "That's all you got to do today?" Waited for him to wake up and said, "You ain't heard from Malik?"

Tiras took the box of chicken from the plastic bag and told himself he would call Malik after he ate, give him some time. Shit, not that Malik hadn't had enough time already, over an hour ago he told him to go drop them two boys off. While he was at Jack Murray's. Pain in the ass having to track this shit down, so much else on his mind at a time like this. He took a scoop of red beans, thinking about the last time he had somebody disposed of close to a major deal of his. At least he told Kwame to shoot that guy first.

This could be different, though, and that bothered him. He'd get Kwame and they'd go to Rudy's after he ate, check it out. Malik and Donny, they could be in there, trying to steal all that dusty old shit Faye likes to hold on to. But still . . .

Tiras took a bite of the chicken, then peeled the skin off and put that in his mouth, cursing himself for breaking one of his rules.

On the way back to the office, Murray watched Miranda, watched her nice rear in black pants. He had seen the hallways once already. That was enough. Back in his chair, Miranda sitting behind the desk across from him, Murray waited for an answer.

"I ran into all of them at Rudy's house," Miranda said. "I was over there, and they came busting in through the back door. Malik isn't talking, neither is his buddy, but the other two looked pretty beat up. You could see that, even though we let them clean up. My guess is that they were going to dump them there. Tiras had to know the house was empty."

"You think that's all they were trying to do?"

"I didn't find any weapons on them. I haven't been able to locate their car yet, but it makes sense. They may have tried to use something in the house. Malik did pull a kitchen knife."

"On *you?*"

"We were in a standoff. I had my gun, so it wasn't much of a duel. I tackled Darnell and put handcuffs on him before that."

"You did that this morning?"

Miranda nodded.

Murray said, "Jesus," in a whisper, then thought about it and said, "What were you doing at Rudy's?"

"Faye called me. They came back to town last night."

"They called you? For what, they working for you as well?"

Miranda shook her head. "No," she said. "Faye wanted more money. She said they got as far as Punta Gorda and turned around and came back wondering if there was anything more I could do to help them."

"What are you going to do?"

"Nothing right now. Tiras is bound to get nervous because if he sent Malik to dump those bodies, he hasn't heard from him yet. He'll go by Rudy's."

"And you're going to let him?"

"I have to, to see how this plays out. Tiras is going to keep bothering him any way you look at it. At least with me involved, it won't be for much longer."

"What if he starts asking about Malik? It's bound to come up."

"I told them to tell him that they've been there all day by themselves. Tiras won't risk his prize possession at this stage.

Hopefully, he'll just let it go. Anyone that could dispute it is in custody." She hesitated for a moment. "That'll only buy so much time, though. I can't keep all of these guys locked in a room forever."

"What else could you do?"

"I could let Malik walk out of here. If I get lucky, he'll take off, stay gone for a while because he's afraid of what Tiras might do. I could have him arraigned. Maybe he has a lawyer. Maybe Tiras takes a chance and posts his bond. He'll get wind of that either way, probably. It might make him nervous enough to call off the whole deal. I don't want that to happen."

"Why not just call him a person of interest, like your boss wants to do with Caesar? You might run the risk of a reprimand, but a guy like that won't want to get into court, air out his business before a jury of his peers. This way you could keep him indefinitely. Even that won't last long because this may wrap up in a day or two."

Murray watched her now, Miranda twisting a ballpoint pen between her fingertips, and kept quiet. He wondered if she liked his idea, the way he was thinking, but got anxious and said, "Are you thinking about it?"

"You know what?" she said, straightening the pen in her hand and pointing it across the desk at him. "That's the best idea I've heard yet."

Tiras believed that looking through a window or knocking on the door would be a waste of time. If somebody would see them, they'd try to hide inside, not answer the door, whatever you do to fool people into thinking you weren't home. He told Kwame to follow him around the side of the house, in the narrow space between the east side of it and a storm fence. Ducking their heads to miss the window unit sticking out.

Tiras stopped cold at the busted back door and turned back

to Kwame. He pushed on it, the door opening crooked on its hinges, and said, "Hello," through the crack. That brought Faye into the kitchen, appearing from the darkened dining area. Coming out of there like some fucking ghost, man, it made Tiras jump. He regained himself and said, "What's going on, girl?"

He smiled at her, but she didn't smile back when she said, "You should try the front door, you come around here."

Tiras didn't say anything to that, kept smiling, and nudged the door open. Held the end of it up with his free hand. "You should get that fixed. Get Rudy to put you up a piece of plywood up there while it's broken."

Faye walked past them and muscled the door back into the frame. "I'll keep it in mind."

Tiras waited for her to do that and come back to stand in front of them before he said, "Maybe I can help him. Where is he?"

Faye said, "You should just ask for him," and turned away from them, not caring if they followed.

Tiras made his way through the dining area, not following Faye around the other way to the living room but knowing that's where she was going. Watching his step in the dark, careful not to trip over boxes that always seemed to be there. Noticing overnight bags on the dining table while he did it. He turned back to Kwame, stepping over boxes, too, and pointed to the bags. Like he was saying, *look at this shit*. They came to the living room, Rudy sitting up in an easy chair, noise from some daytime talk show in the background. Tiras saw Rudy look at him then down at the pistol in Tiras's waistband, Tiras's t-shirt pulled back to let him see it. Something he put there to help Rudy make up his mind.

"Y'all went on a trip?" Tiras said.

Rudy was quiet, rubbing his forehead.

Tiras said, "Was it fun?"

Neither Rudy nor Faye said anything to that, and Tiras didn't really care if they did or not. In the same breath, he said, "I was telling Faye you should take a look at your back door. It's all fucked up. You need to get somebody to fix it for you."

"That was my fault," Faye said, "on account of I forgot the house key. Rudy had to jimmy the door, bust it in so's we could get inside."

"Rudy's an old pro at that," Tiras said. "It don't look like the work of a veteran burglar like him." He stopped and thought. "How you gonna leave on a trip and not take your house key?"

Faye watched Kwame laughing and shrugged. "It happens."

"Not to people with half-a-fucking brain, it don't." Tiras moved across the living room, passed slow in front of the TV to piss Faye off and stood next to Rudy's chair. He said, "Y'all been here all morning? By yourself?"

Rudy shifted in his chair. He knew what was coming and nodded, hoping it would be enough.

"Ain't nobody come over to see you?"

Rudy said, "We been here since last night. Got back from Punta Gorda about midnight. Faye's been up for a while. I just woke up."

"Punta Gorda, huh?" Tiras said. "Sounds like you had a good time."

Tiras stayed calm, telling himself it was okay. *He sees you have a gun. It's right there in his face.* But it was getting hard to stay that way. This one-way conversation had him feeling like he was being jerked around.

He said, "You know we got some business left," starting to lose it. "How come you gonna up and leave like that?"

"We needed to get away, that's all," Rudy said. "I was going to call you, but we ended up coming back instead."

"When were you going to call me? You been back since last

night, I got to come over here and find you sitting around watching TV."

Rudy said, "Lloyd's probably in town by now," anxious to change the subject.

"I expect he is. You better hope he didn't decide to leave."

That was something Rudy hadn't thought about, his conversation change going nowhere. Fucking Tiras, you couldn't talk to him about anything without him throwing something in your face. Okay, so it was fucked up. Get over it. Rudy thought, *If it wasn't for me, you wouldn't even know about Lloyd Bone, willing to pay your price for some cheap piece of shit guns.* He thought about telling Tiras something but stopped.

Tiras said, "C'mon, get up."

Rudy said, "Where we going?"

"We gonna try and straighten this out. You going to make a call so we can set up a time."

Rudy got up without saying a word, without so much as grabbing a toothbrush, and turned for the door.

On their way out, by the time he was on the front porch, Tiras could hear Faye saying, "Hey, I thought you were gonna help us with the back door?"

Outside, Tiras put his shades on and straightened his Kangol. Ready to get out of this goddamn neighborhood. Shit, the fucking watch on his wrist cost more than some of the cars around here.

He had his hand on Rudy's back, walking him down the cement walkway that led to the street, Kwame flanking Rudy's other side, gazing up and down the block like they were the secret service.

Thinking about cars before, Tiras could've sworn he recognized Malik's El Dorado, white with the dark tint, parked down the street. He looked twice and, yeah, it even had the eight ball curb feelers.

Driving home, Murray kept seeing Miranda sitting across the desk from him, telling him how the caper would go. That's the word he used to himself, caper. She looked different to him in an office. Not the same way he imagined her the first time, back when her name was Shelly Suxxx, waking up in her panties and his shirt. Shelly Suxxx? Where did she get that? Maybe her boss, making it sound like he had something for her.

She seemed a long way from that now.

Now, he saw her as more officious than anything. He remembered that word from an old movie and decided it fit her. Like the way she went through exactly what would happen, like she had seen this all before with some knucklehead criminal she had put under investigation before. Telling him every step Tiras would make before he would make it.

Was she doing the same thing with him? Just not saying it out loud?

He thought the Rudy situation was pretty cold. Letting him stew, knowing Tiras was going back over there. Using him. It almost made Murray feel sorry for Rudy, the guy unaccustomed to the type of dudes he was dealing with now. Maybe Tiras was already there.

Was she using him, too? If she was, he wouldn't know it.

How about when he mentioned what to do with Malik? Jumping all over that. He thought she liked his thinking about that. Didn't say as much but Malik was still there when he left. He remembered her saying that it was the best idea she'd heard. It made him wonder why she hadn't thought of it before.

Murray didn't say anything about it, but did ask her if she thought she could get in trouble. She said, "If this doesn't go right, I might be looking for a job."

Sounding serious about it. Like it could actually happen.

He asked her if she was serious, and she said yes. Then he said, "Maybe you shouldn't do it."

She said, "You're probably right. But, I'm going to anyway, provided it's not too long." Then, stopped and looked at him for what seemed like forever, and said, "You and I are going to have to cool it for a while, though." Getting around to it.

He didn't say anything, just nodded, and wondered if he did wrong. Maybe she wanted him to object, put up some kind of fight. He couldn't tell. He was still thinking about it, wandering off while watching windshields and headlights in lanes going the other way down Collins Avenue.

While he was silent, she said, "You okay with that?" Probing. He wasn't sure what he was with it at first. When she said, "Because that's something I know I can get into trouble for," Murray knew he should go along.

Sure he was okay with it. Now. As much as he was sure with the fact that they were all business at this point. The suspense gone from that. Her business card. The cell phone.

No doubt about it.

The question was, what would they be from here? He tried to be realistic about it. The last time he did that, the night they went to Mac's, she ended up in his bed. That wasn't going to happen again. He looked at it from her vantage point. The same thing he did before. He could go at it over and over. What was the point? There's a reason the old saying goes 'you can't have your cake and eat it, too.' Nope, you had to make a choice.

It was seven P.M. when Murray called Tiras, ready to say that he couldn't get in touch with Rudy, give some excuse.

When Tiras said, "I got him. Get over here," it surprised him. Not shock because he had prepared himself for the possibility. He was told it would happen.

She was right.

Seven-thirty, Murray and Nicky Silva, in Nicky's Maxima, pulled up in Tiras's driveway. Nicky with that annoying habit of dropping in without calling first. Not that Murray had a number to call, but still.

Inside, no one paying them any mind, Murray and Nicky watched Tiras and Kwame walking back and forth, handling a different gun each time they appeared. Lil' Man and Rudy sitting with them in the living room, staring off into space. Tiras came into the living room, handed Lil' Man a gun and disappeared again.

Murray said, "We don't get one?"

"No, you don't," Tiras said, coming from the back of the house, checking a magazine on a .45. "And, if you got something on, you put it on the table."

Tiras looked down at Murray, sitting across the coffee table on the sofa. "Stand up," he said. "Lil' Man going to search you, make sure you clean."

Murray gave Tiras a look and didn't move. "What the hell are you talking about, search us?" Tiras racked the slide on his .45, and Murray gave Nicky a look, shaking his head. He stood up and felt Lil' Man pat him down, softly, like his heart wasn't in it. Murray watched Lil' Man feel around the outside of his pants pocket and saw his hand go in there. He pulled out Murray's cell phone.

"What you got that for?" Tiras said, walking over to inspect. "Leave that here."

Murray wondered if he could do that or not, leave government property in a criminal's house. He did it anyway, asked Tiras if he was done, sat down and watched them do the same thing to Nicky Silva; Lil' Man pulling a .38 out of Nicky's waistband, at the small of his back, emptying the chamber and throwing it on the coffee table.

Murray looked at his watch. "Almost eight already. Why don't we get started? I want to get home."

Tiras said, "You ain't going anywhere soon."

"What're you going to do?" Murray said. "Make us some dinner?"

"We gonna do this shit right now. Tonight." He watched Murray's reaction. Saw Murray give a look to Nicky and said, "Yeah, some things have happened to where I got to move my timetable up. Made a call this afternoon. My buyer's in town. I arranged for delivery at ten o'clock, so we just gonna go do this. Got this spot picked out, a field off Federal Highway. Up there, across from the Fort Lauderdale airport, where the old drive-in used to be."

"How'd you swing that?" Murray said, glancing down at his phone.

Tiras said, "I owe that to my man, Rudy," slapping Rudy on the back. "He did me a favor, decided to help me out, being the good friend that he is. Man was already in town. Ready to go home, actually." He said to Rudy, "Thank God you came back from vacation, huh?"

Tiras moved his attention back to Murray. He said, "And it's going to happen just like I told you this morning, Mister Jack. You, Rudy and your man here gonna stand next to each other, lined up, two crates of machine guns in front of you. You going to open one up, let him see he getting what he suppose to be getting. Then, he going to give you a bag of money. You don't do nothing with that. You give that to me."

Nicky said, "Where are you going to be?"

"I going to be around, chief. Don't worry about that. I may not be right there with you, but I'll be there. Your buddy here say he want half even though we been doing all the work, so he going to work for it. He do that, he get half. I ain't going to sit around arguing about it. I'm a man of my word. You want your money, you talk to him. Now, Mister Jack, I'm going to be telling you how to do some things, how I want them done, you see? I don't want you to take no offense, like I'm bossing you. I just have ways I like things done, and I know what I'm doing. You follow what I tell you, we'll be back here cutting up the cash. After that, you on your way 'cause we ain't going to want to see each other again. What else . . . ?"

Nicky said, "How about your guys? Where are they going to be?"

"They going to be with me, wherever I am. Look, man, I don't know where you come from, but you just need to worry about staying close to your boss. You do that, you be okay."

"He's not my boss."

Nicky looked at Murray. Murray shrugged. Tiras watched.

He said, "That's between y'all."

Seven thirty-five, Miranda had gotten a call that a black Nissan Maxima was at Tiras's house, two white males in the car.

Ten minutes later, enough time to get some clothes on and grab her gear, she was headed up there, up to Tiras's house to see firsthand what was going on, expecting the worst, wondering why she hadn't heard about this from Jack.

Chapter Nineteen

Murray thought about his government-issue cell phone sitting on Tiras's living room coffee table and saw his life go before his eyes. Not calling Miranda when he had the chance was his mistake, not wanting to call with Nicky Silva right there, like a shadow, thinking he would be able to call when he got back home, talk about the events of the evening, where to take it from there. But, there wasn't any going home. The cavalry wasn't coming, either. No, just him playing out the string in the backseat of a Cadillac Escalade wedged between Nicky and Lil' Man, preferring to think of Lil' Man as Marion Williams right now. Tiras was driving with Rudy in the front passenger seat and the merchandise in the rear cab. Kwame was driving Nicky's Maxima, somewhere behind them.

Turning off onto Sunrise, Tiras was speaking his hip-hop language, one all his own to the beats of whatever it was coming through the speakers. Something none of them could understand except maybe Lil' Man picking up on some of it. Murray watched and listened, realizing that it was the same old shit he had been through too many times before, just with different faces this time. Going somewhere fucked up in the middle of the night to do something fucked up. Always zigging when he should have zagged. Putting himself in this position, his own worst enemy. He'd hear Nicky say something, sometimes out loud; something that would have had some oomph to it around his crowd, goombahs standing around a street corner. Something that wasn't working here.

Going east on Sunrise before veering onto Federal Highway, Tiras was on the phone with Kwame, telling him, "No, you going to hang back in that car. We going to come back and sit with you. You watch for me when I get off the road." Having to repeat it while Kwame turned down the Maxima's stereo. Nicky told Tiras, "That fucker better not do anything to my car. I'll kill him before we leave here if he does." That got Tiras looking in the rearview mirror. Not saying anything, just giving a knowing look. Nicky said, "He better not fuck with my stations, either. I get in there and find that rap shit on, I'll kill him for that, too." They passed the Fort Lauderdale airport, Lil' Man and Murray watching floodlights, planes coming and going through tinted windows, slowing down before turning off into an empty parking lot, rows of corrugated aluminum buildings on one end, an industrial park, continuing past into a grassy field beyond that.

They settled into a spot about two hundred yards from the edge of the parking lot, away from the streetlights. All five of them were out of the Escalade, trying to get crates out of the rear cab, clumsy about it, weight shifting back and forth between whoever was on either end. "Easy," they heard Tiras say. Murray looked at him. Hell no, there wasn't anything easy about it. It was fucking hard, dealing with this shit for you. "You drop that," Tiras said, "I drop you." He started grabbing people and moving them, saying, "I want y'all over here," pointing to a spot a couple of feet behind the crates. "Rudy, you going to be out front because Lloyd knows you."

Rudy said, "Wait, you're not going to be here?"

"No, you tell the man I got a, what do you call it, previous engagement. Yeah, I got something else to do. You handlin' this deal for me."

With that, Tiras gave some more orders. "Make damn sure you see the money. He open up the bag, you look inside. That's all you do."

Murray said, "You don't want it counted?"

"What you gonna do, lay it out in the grass and look it over, a thousand at a time in little stacks?" Tiras laughed. "Shit no, man. He short me, we'll find him. Rudy gonna help me with that if he needs to. My guess is he going to see what a operator I am, sending my people to do this, he'll do right."

Murray said, "What are we supposed to do?"

"You just stand there, you suppose to be the backup, the muscle. Although muscle like you don't make me look too good, I have to say. Rudy going to hand the bag to you—after he see inside—and you just stand there, holding it."

Tiras kept going, doing what he said he was going to do. Tell them what to do, trying not to boss them. He finished, double-checked with Rudy, and jumped into the front of the Escalade.

Later, after they had watched the bulky Cadillac motor around the side of the first warehouse, Nicky said, "What are we doing here?"

"You heard him," Murray said, "we're the muscle."

Across the highway, on the airport side, Miranda and Special Agents Phelps and Taylor watched the field. Moving binoculars back and forth from a dark space where the black Escalade was to the spot where it ended up—behind a nearby warehouse parked next to a black Maxima.

Taylor said, "What's going on over there?"

"A gun deal," Miranda said, matter of fact. "An unknown number of automatic weapons to be exchanged for an unknown amount of cash, probably in the six figures, maybe close to three hundred grand."

The agents looked at each other.

Some time passed, almost half an hour by the car dashboard clock, the three of them making small talk. The guys asking Miranda about her personal life, her not answering some of their questions. Pretty sure one of them was going to ask her out for drinks. The clock read 9:48 P.M. when a Suburban turned off the road and headed for the field.

"This is it," Miranda said, taking the binoculars off the warehouse and putting them on the tail end of the Chevy. She saw it stop at the edge of the parking lot, engine idling, headlights going to high beam. Figures appeared in the light, off in the distance. The beams went back to low, and the Suburban moved forward.

Phelps said, "Gimme the number."

Miranda read what she could get off the plate while Phelps was on a small laptop. She watched the Suburban circle around, cut its lights and come to a stop.

Miranda heard Phelps from the backseat say, "The partial matches the numbers off a Ford pickup in Marietta, reported three days ago." She watched the two groups almost squaring off, sizing up the other side in a situation like this. She recognized Jack. Also recognized Rudy and the other white guy, the one Jack introduced as Nick. The others, two black guys. She could tell which one was Lloyd Bone: mid- to late-thirties, maybe early forties, about six foot, one-seventy, dark shirt, dark slacks. Talking and smiling with Rudy. She was quiet, watching Lloyd's second open his jacket to show a gun.

"How do you want to handle this?" Taylor said amid the sound of bulletproof vests being fastened and pistol chambers being loaded.

"We're going to take them down," Miranda said. She watched the scene in the field, a bag passed from Lloyd to Rudy, the top of one of the wood crates still open, the lid propped up against the side of the box. It gave her time to call the Florida Department of Law Enforcement for backup. She moved the binoculars to the warehouse area, looking twice to make sure what she saw: Tiras Williams and his crew, crouched behind their cars, loading guns.

"We'll start in the parking lot."

What Kwame was loading, and what he showed to Lil' Man, was a chunky .357, already with a Glock tucked into his pants. Lil' Man asked could he hold it. Kwame gave it to him then went for his other .357, one lying on the ground next to him. "You wanna use it?" Kwame said. "Man, you blow somebody in half with that thing." Lil' Man flipped it over in his hand, the weight feeling good to him. He moved his arm up and down, gauging the feel, looking down the sight. Hell yeah, he wanted to use it. He stared down the sight again, did that watching Kwame stooped behind the Nissan, making hand signals back and forth with Tiras. Then, he moved the sight to the back of Kwame's head and thought about it.

Nah, get him to turn around. Look that motherfucker in the eye when you do it.

"We got a gun, the fat kid right there," Taylor said.

They drove up into the parking lot, taking a sharp left toward the industrial park where Taylor saw the fat kid turn his head. The kid looked at them, like he wasn't expecting them but knew who they were. He hesitated for a moment deciding what to do.

What the kid decided to do was unload on a guy behind the black Maxima parked in front of them. That guy dropped instantly, lying still under the double exhaust sticking out from under the rear bumper.

"Drop that gun," Phelps said, moving out from the rear of the agents' car. "I'm not fucking around with you."

The kid didn't do anything but had to hear Miranda tell him the same thing. Had to hear Taylor, too, right in front of him. But what he did was turn what they could see was a .357 on himself.

Put in right under his chin and pulled the trigger.

"What the fuck is that shit?"

Murray heard Lloyd Bone say that and grabbed Rudy. Got him—and the bag—out of there, fast as they could run in the opposite direction. Murray looked back, although he told himself not to, and saw Lloyd Bone jumping into his truck. Nicky Silva right behind them, staying close to him and Rudy. Then, he looked beyond Nicky and saw the Suburban fishtailing in the middle of the field, looking for a way out.

Nicky said, "What the fuck happened?"

Murray shrugged and wondered what would happen to the two wood boxes sitting there. He turned to Rudy and said, "You know what happened?"

Rudy's eyes were wide, Murray's words not registering. After a moment, he shrugged. Everybody shrugging right now.

Nicky said, "What now?"

Murray looked around, settling on a spot to the east, towards the water. "We should get moving. Seventh Avenue should be that way, maybe we can get a cab." He patted the bag hanging in his left hand. "We got plenty of money."

Special Agent Phelps said, "I see another one over there."

He watched Miranda slide around the side of the Maxima. She looked over the roof at the Escalade parked less than a hundred feet away, trying to figure out where Tiras was and saw a shadow from the streetlight above.

Tiras was hiding behind the rear driver's side wheel well.

She said to Phelps, "Stay where you are. Talk to him."

Phelps nodded while Taylor was on the radio.

Phelps said, "Come out from behind there, give yourself up. Nobody wants to get hurt."

Tiras said, "Fuck that shit," and let out a round from a shotgun that shattered against the government Chevrolet parked at the edge of the warehouse.

Miranda heard sirens in the distance for the first time and felt Tiras starting to get nervous. She didn't want to have to chase him. Especially in heels. You could get seriously hurt running around, not knowing where you were going. Maybe Tiras does know, he picked this place.

Miranda started moving to the front of the Nissan, crouching lower the further she got along the hood of the car, her nine-millimeter held against her leg. She heard Phelps yelling for Tiras to give himself up again, saw Tiras's head pop up, trying to find him through that fucking super-dark tinted glass. Something you couldn't see through normally except for the overhead lights tonight. She heard Phelps yelling again, keeping Tiras occupied; maybe too occupied. Tiras got off another shot, Miranda hearing it hit the building behind them. A loud fucking clank on the side of it. Then, she heard the shotgun hit the cement. He was either digging out more shells or switching to something else. Miranda took that time to step the twenty yards or so to the front grill of the Escalade. She thought Tiras might have heard her but knew he didn't when Tiras said, "Where that fuckin' bitch at?" She saw Tiras's head start to turn and stepped out in front of him. She could make out a .44 in his hand and squeezed off two rounds, center mass. Tiras hit the rear panel of his Cadillac, rolled over on the end of the bumper sticking out and hit the ground. She kept her pistol on him while she approached.

Miranda kicked the .44 out from Tiras's hand and wondered where Jack was.

Murray had put Rudy in the bedroom, passed out from nerves. He passed out in the cab on the way back. Made the cab ride quiet, at least, none of them saying anything. Just what they needed at that time, a little peace and quiet to get thoughts together. Rudy's limp body got Faye hysterical when they walked through her front door, thinking he was dead.

Murray said, "He'll just sleep it off," and closed the door. He started to tell Faye what happened when Nicky asked if she had a phone he could use to call a friend to come pick him up. She said, yeah, long as it wasn't long distance. He said it was his girlfriend—not that she had asked that—and that it was local; Gina staying in a hotel in Delray Beach.

As Nicky took the phone into the kitchen, Faye said to Murray, "What are you gonna do now?"

"I'm going to call Miranda so she can come and get the money." Anxious to do that. He thought about what was going through her mind right now, where she was. All this commotion, not realizing that he didn't have her number on him, not wanting to carry her card this evening.

Faye saw that look on Murray's face and said, "Lemme get you her number."

Murray waited while Faye shuffled off to the bedroom. He looked toward the kitchen, the light on in there, and wondered when Nicky was going to be finished with his call.

Nicky was talking to Gina, trying to give her directions to get to him from where she was. He thought it was pretty easy, just use 95, but Gina was getting confused, in a state. He yelled back to the living room a couple of times for direction from Faye for once she got off the interstate.

"What are you doing there?" Gina said.

"Everything was fucked up. This is where we ended up."

"What happened?"

He didn't feel like getting into it. Just said, "Somebody started shooting. We still don't know who. My guess is it's somebody Tiras pissed off, wanted to fuck the whole thing up and get something for himself. Lucky we didn't get *our* heads blown off, dealing with somebody like that."

"Where's the money?"

"It's here."

Nicky gave Gina the directions for once she got off the interstate and told her to repeat them back to make sure she got them right. Then, he asked her if the Toyota she had was still running okay, barely making it from Caesar's house to the hotel two days ago. Not telling her about his car yet. His car. Shit, that was another thing.

Gina's voice over the phone said, "Baby, you know I keep a little pistol in my handbag? Something Caesar gave me one time. You think you can use it?"

Chapter Twenty

Miranda drove Nicky's car over. The Chevrolet the agents had was all busted up now, first by a round from Tiras's shotgun—that wasn't too bad, you could still drive it—second, when one of the agents, she couldn't tell which at the time, took out Lloyd Bone's driver as they were trying to get out of the warehouse parking lot. Got off a lucky shot and hit the guy's right shoulder. He lost control and *bam,* the guy skidded right into them.

Now, cruising down 95, Miranda thought about what she could tell her boss about what happened tonight. Oh, as long as he saw a headline that started with "Federal agents seize . . ." and his name was mentioned prominently, he'd be okay. She dismissed that from her mind and thought about Jack. She'd try to keep him out of it; she'd done a good job of it so far. She was glad when he called, the first thing he said was, "Are you okay?" Showing concern for her.

Then, she said, "Where are you?"

He said they were at Rudy's and that's where she got worried, judging the time difference from where they were. They could get a head start if they decided to leave, about an hour. They wouldn't get far but that wasn't the point.

Then he told her what happened: that he didn't have his phone on him, that he didn't expect to be out there tonight—having to explain things to her that didn't make him look like a crook.

She approached Rudy's street and called the house. To be

sure they were still there, maybe something had changed. She tried twice to no answer. She turned onto Sixty-ninth and saw a Toyota double-parked in front of Rudy's house, hazard lights going on and off in the night.

Miranda checked the magazine on her nine-millimeter and got out of the car.

There were footsteps beyond the front door. Murray said, "She's here."

Nicky said, "Somebody open the door. Don't look so damned suspicious."

Faye moved for it, she and Miranda smiling at each other.

Miranda looked inside, a lot of people in there, at least four that she could see. Like she was late for a party.

Murray watched Miranda adjust her pistol in a holster on her hip, keeping a hand on it.

Nicky said, "What do you need that for?"

"You never know," Miranda said, looking at the blonde next to Nick. "Who's that?"

She watched the blonde while Nick told her the girl's name, Gina. Miranda waited, keeping an eye on those two, and turned to Murray. "Where's the money?"

He pointed to a bag across the room from him, a brown leather bag sitting on the chair next to where Nick was standing.

Miranda jumped when the bedroom door opened. But, it was only Rudy coming out, a sleepy look on his face. She watched Rudy, who gave her a nod, make his way to the living room sofa. She looked at Murray and said, "How much is in there?"

He said, "Should be about a quarter million. I haven't counted it, though."

She nodded, slowly, like she was thinking, then said, "I'm going to need statements from whoever was there," and looked around the room at men nodding, eager to help her out.

Murray saw Miranda start to reach for the bag and watched Nicky begin to go into the hip pocket of his leather coat. He said, "Nicky's got a gun!" with some force, raising his voice to get Miranda's attention, making sure she heard him. Murray saw Nicky's head swivel towards him for a moment—anger on his face—Murray thinking that it was a dumb move to do that just then.

A dumb move because the look on Nicky's face changed to surprise when he looked back around. Miranda had her pistol on him. She saw Nicky tugging at his coat pocket, trying to get it out of there, and got off a round in Nicky's chest. Got off a second one when he kept coming, finally getting that .38 out from his pocket, and then it was over.

Murray let out a big breath after.

Miranda walked over to Nicky's body, laying in the corner behind a recliner, and felt for a pulse. She looked up at the blonde whose name she couldn't remember, crying now, and said, "This your boyfriend?" and watched the girl nod. "You know he had a gun?"

Before the blonde could answer, Faye said, "That bitch gave it to him. It was in her purse."

Miranda sat the girl down and let her let it out. She looked at Faye and said, "You remember you were wondering if there was anything more I could do for you?"

"Yes, ma'am, I do."

"How about giving you and Rudy your lives back. Is that enough?"

Miranda said, "You're really taking off, huh?"

"Yeah, it's well past time."

"What are you going to do?"

"I don't know. I have some family in New Jersey I haven't

seen in a long time. I might head up there, say hello."

"New Jersey?"

"I didn't say I was staying."

Miranda watched Jack packing up some things into an old gym bag, a weird combination of regret and optimism coming over her.

He said, "I saw you made the paper yesterday, the front page."

"Yeah, but below the fold. My supervisor called to yell at somebody about that, but I don't know what happened. You were the 'unidentified informant.' "

"I figured as much. Just make sure you tell my parole officer."

She said, "It's already done," and stopped, not smiling anymore. Just watching. "You know I'm probably going to get a promotion out of this. I'm definitely taking a transfer back to my old boss, Bill Cecil."

"You excited about that?"

She nodded. "And, I wanted to thank you for the help you gave me."

"Hey, we both made out. You get a promotion and maybe a spiffy new office; I get a second chance. If anything, I should be thanking you."

Miranda had a feeling she had missed something. She smiled at Jack, watching the energy he was using in folding his shirts and throwing them in his bag. She said, "How are you getting a second chance?"

"I just am, don't worry."

She let it go and said, "You think you'll come back?"

"Sure, but I need to get away, collect myself." Sure, he would be back, hoping she would still be there, too, resigned for the time being that it wasn't going to work for one reason or another, surprised it got this far. If he came back in six months or a year, whenever . . . well, then maybe they were meant for something more.

Miranda said, "Jack, can I ask you something?" Sounding like a question but really telling him. "There was just under two hundred-fifty thousand in the bag."

"That's what I told you, about a quarter million."

She moved close to him, and he saw the corners of her mouth turn up and her eyes begin to sparkle. "Shouldn't there have been more?"

ABOUT THE AUTHOR

Brandon Hebert lives in a sleepy south Louisiana town with his wife, Carmen, and two high-maintenance dogs, Lucy and Lily. In his spare time, he enjoys being at home, fishing with his dad, relaxing with family and friends, and dissecting fake Cajun accents in movies.

Please visit him at www.brandonhebert.com.